Burnt Christians

Helen Mirth

The following title by Helen Mirth will be available Spring 2012:
Side Effects of Money

Published by TBT Publisher
Photo by staff
Copyright 2012

All rights reserved
Printed in the United States of America
Please request permission from author before reproducing this material in any way.

For more information
or to purchase products
contact us at:

info@TBTpublisher.com
TBT Publisher
P.O. Box 502
Mount Dora, FL 32756

ISBN: 978-0-9837687-5-3

For
the pursuit of sanity and light,
I wish you all the best.

Table of Contents

Introduction

Part 1

Chapter 1-The Eccentric Bette 2

Chapter 2- Escape From Hank's Village 11

Part 2

Chapter 3- The First Descent 27

Chapter 4- A Vicious Streak of Crazy 39

Chapter 5-The (Not So) Little Bette 47

Chapter 6- Bette In Love 66

Chapter 7- The First Flash Light 73

Chapter 8- The Neem Leaf Conflict 80

Chapter 9- The Madison Trip Down 89

Chapter 10- Brain Crystal Phone Battle 114

Chapter 11-Neem Compromise Plumb 121

Part 3

Chapter 12- The 3rd Ceramic Rant 136

Chapter 13- Epsom Salt Catalyst War 159

Chapter 14- The 'Do Over' Revolution 173

Chapter 15- Going Back for Her 190

Chapter 16- St. Mary's Haven 215

Chapter 17- A Good Catholic Mother 229

Chapter 18- Why She Left Home 243

Chapter 19- Shutting Out the Light 255

Part 4

Chapter 20- Burnt Christians 265

Chapter 21- Hemlock And Curry 288

Chapter 22 –Angel of Death 309

Introduction

In *Burnt Christians*, Mirth tells a compelling purgatory tale reminiscent of Flannery O'Conner, in which she explores the themes of madness, memory, guilt, and failures of family.

The protagonist, June Marie, takes her elderly and quietly hostile mother into her care. Spurred by her mother's alternately mad and manipulative ways, June embarks on an existential journey in which she delves into her own past to root out the source of her mother's madness, her own cumbersome sense of filial piety, and their resultant disharmony.

As the novel's heart, June is deeply sympathetic, human, and unafraid to lay bare the tender places of memory. She stands in stark contrast to the mother, who is charged with a bizarre and shifting madness and who fails to allow herself to be changed by life, instead futilely seeking to control reality by crafting her perception of it.

Margaret Christ

Part 1

Chapter 1
The Eccentric Bette

In my dream, Dr. Phil told me that when someone dies from itching they go to purgatory. He and his helper Christian would make sure of it. Then as he reviewed my mother's medical file he said that she would die if I failed to explain why the rose bush was *mortally* pruned.

Before I had a chance to defend myself, the phone rang and I fumbled in the dark to reach it.

It was Mom and she said she was dying. That's when I was suddenly wide awake. "Why!" I whispered fearfully. "What happened?"

She sobbed that her itching was so bad she had to go around with no clothes! It was 28 degrees in Wisconsin, so she knew she would freeze to death.

I offered no alternatives.

My 84 year old mother is normally not crazy. She is not on any drugs and she is not senile.

Yet, she had been claiming for about six months that 'aphid critters' were hiding in her clothes. She said they came out to feed on her skin cells and made her itch all over.

This is what made her run away from her 'infested' apartment. She then tried to live with each of my twelve siblings in rotation.

The longest stay lasted two weeks, the shortest two hours, and that was with Christian, my second oldest brother and her favorite child.

She avoided staying with me because the ride to Florida was too long.

I wasn't sure where she was calling from, but it was 3 a.m., and she was probably naked.

I started the family phone tree to warn everyone that the saga was resuming.

After someone had rescued Mom, I was called to attend the emergency family meeting via phone.

It turned into a kind of veteran's support group. Each of my siblings had their turn to speak of the misery of living with Mom, especially the midnight runs to the emergency room for 'itching induced' false alarms.

I thought they were exaggerating.

I liked Mom because I had mostly fond memories of her.

Of course, those memories were old ones, from before she had gotten so 'eccentric', from before Dad died twenty years ago.

I recalled that shortly after he died, Mom turned our house into a sort of commune for needy people. She called them 'helpers'.

She had a steady stream of 'helpers' for about four years, until one woman actually sued Mom for $2,000.

Mom was accused of neglect. She failed to warn anyone about the cat which the woman was severely allergic to. Mom's defense was that she didn't know she had a cat.

It never went to court because Mom just gave the woman the money.

The news of this generous payout got around and Mom was swamped with requests to join her 'commune'. It turned into a communist nightmare.

To escape, she moved to an Ashram outside Chicago, which was really another commune. Yet it was the nicest place she had ever lived outside of home.

For five years the communists took good care of Mom. They even took her to a 'time share' in India for a few months that had '24-hour access to a swami'.

Sadly, the communists eventually asked Mom to leave. Mom explained that it was really political infighting which forced her out.

For many years she wandered from one group of communists to another, like a religious nomad.

She'd call from mysterious places with odd requests. "I'm here in Norwich. Soon the soy will be foul. Bring a better bag."

It took some code-breaking to figure that this meant that she was ready at the Norwich Avenue train station, but that her soybean soup was spoiling and leaking out of the disposable bag she preferred to store it in. So could we bring a better container?

In addition to odd food, she had a network of curious 'helpers' that she would stay with or who would sometimes travel with her.

Finally, a few years ago, some of those helpers persuaded her to stay in a tiny place they had found for her. Mike and Mark, our twin brothers, helped her move.

Their voices over the phone brought me back to the present dilemma. I could hear them finishing up their story. They were joking about how they almost got arrested for helping her plant all that 'weed'.

Rowdy laughter burst from the phone. My family was having a good time, as we always did.

Mom knew that the marijuana plants were illegal, but she maintained that octogenarians should be above the law. She also claimed that 'pot' was 'medicine' for her 'friends', the vegetables which she grew mostly for Christian, who sometimes lived in her basement. He was kind of eccentric too.

She got annoyed with him though because he was strongly opposed to the illegal plants, and especially to the kind of 'helpers' they attracted.

She was getting such a reputation that some of the 'helpers' were camping in her tiny yard, waiting for the 'pot' to be ready. Christian hated that. It's why he boycotted the marijuana.

This alone was not too problematic because he was good to her in other ways, like supporting her choice to wash dishes with seaweed.

However he got nervous about sleeping in the same house with the counter-top ceramic fire pits that she used for cooking and heating. Since she wouldn't stop, he insisted that we steal the rags she used to feed the fire. We agreed of course, but she was sharp enough to notice that her rags were missing. When she found that the weed had been uprooted, she was furious and told Christian to leave or she would.

He didn't so she did. No one could stop her.

Probably out of spite, she found an apartment above a drug lord. She claims she picked it only because it was next to an historic basilica, where she could attend daily Mass.

Of course, we didn't know for sure that he was a drug lord until a news flash reported that he got shot down on the front steps of the beautiful church, right after mass. Mom was a witness and was even interviewed about it.

Christian called some of my siblings *demanding* that we *make* her move to a safer apartment. It was an impossible scheme because Mom was *not* a movable person, especially because she was indifferent to danger. She believed she was safe because they were not aiming at her.

Fortunately she did move, but not because of organized crime. The itch drove her out.

That was about six months ago.

That was when she started her path of destruction through the lives of each of her kids. I was the exception.

A home for the elderly was preferable to living with me. That's why she moved into Hank's Village.

At Hank's Village, she happily agreed to have blood and urine tests done to determine what was making her itch, and if it was fatal.

All they found was an allergy to soy and a lack of vitamin D. She had nothing physically life threatening, or even anything to make her sick.

Of course she insisted that the doctors were wrong, but we didn't worry about her dying.

However several siblings insisted Mom was a lunatic. After a few weeks of assisting Mom's living, the staff of Hank's Village agreed.

Mom insisted that the critters were colonizing the fabric of everything in her apartment, and would spread to the whole structure.
She politely asked the staff for a lighter so she could burn her clothes and anything else that was infested. They said no fires were allowed inside the building.
It was Mom's final solution to not wear clothes at all which persuaded Hank's Village to evict her.
The manager called my brother Paul and explained politely that 'the board' decided that Mom was a bad influence on the elderly.

So, after just 10 weeks, our Mother got kicked out of assisted living.

Chapter 2
Escape From Hank's Village

At first no one was concerned that Hank's Village rejected our mother. She had until the end of the month, and there were other care places, or so we thought.

We soon learned that Mom had earned a reputation for being eccentric and rebellious. None of the local assisted living communities wanted her.

We were prepared to challenge that assessment, but then didn't have to.

Mom vowed to never set foot in another nursing home again.

It was useless to explain the difference between a *nursing home* and *assisted living*. To her they were equally tyrannical and unenlightened.

To our chagrin, she also vowed not to stay in Hank's Village *one more minute*.

She called every one of us, including me, pleading to come and get her 'out of jail'.

None of us slept that night as our phones buzzed with panicked discussion about Mom.

Christian was with her at Hank's and could see she was bent on running away, naked, into the freezing cold night. He was afraid he could not stop her, and something had to be done immediately. He even offered to take her somewhere else himself.

But Christian had never gotten a driver's license, for political reasons. Therefore, his offer to 'take her somewhere else' meant he would carry Mom away on the back of his bicycle.

No one said it to him, but Christian's solutions were always more like a threat that provoked us to action. To me they were like a nightmare. This was no exception. I imagined the bizarre bicycle-taxi scenario playing out on the icy dark streets of the city.

Our brother Mark was quickly pressed to intervene because he was one of the twin babies and so could persuade her with his charm.

He agreed to take her to one of her many generous but mentally unstable friends.

The first friend was wide awake at 3 a.m. and happy for Mom's visit. Mom pleasantly explained how mad Hank's Village was about the fact that she couldn't wear clothes anymore. The friend nodded with understanding and said "I've always said, Bette, that the Wisconsin medical system is very oppressive. Come in and have some tea."

Everything seemed fine until Mom explained sweetly, "I only need Olive oil sponge baths every few hours because those skin eating critters hate Olive oil."

She lasted there for just under 40 minutes, the shortest stay ever.

Mark had to drive Mom around the city to seek out the other friends but she was rejected by everyone for exactly the same reasons.

While he drove her to a hotel, Mom complained about her friends having a

problem with nudity.
Mark snapped, "They have a problem with giving you sponge baths! Why can't you just take a shower?"

She started to sob about how she just wanted to go back to the old ways where everyone helped each other. Mark got mad and told her she needed help. That made Mom suddenly furious and she snapped, "I'm 84! There is something eating me alive and I don't need any of you! Except for sponge baths in the places I can't reach or see! And is that so much to ask of my own children?! I gave them life! What do I get in return?!"

Mark tried to set her straight, "Life is not a deal you make with your kids! And your friends are not your kids anyway."
"Yeah! " She scoffed. "At least my friends want me to be free like they are. You kids just want to control me! Christian is always telling me I can't plant weeds."

Mark gave up because Mom was getting so irrational.

They had been driving around for hours and it was already sunrise.

He finally made her stay at a hotel for the day, and insisted she keep her clothes on. She was too exhausted to argue.

Later in the afternoon he took her to the mental evaluation appointment one of our siblings had set up.

The results of the evaluation were immediate and Mark was able to give us the news that night.

Unfortunately, it was not good.

The doctor stated that Mom was still very sharp for her age, for any age and had no signs of mental incompetence.

We were all incredulous that professional doctors had labeled our mother as officially '*not* crazy'. It was as if they had not met her.

Mark explained that apparently she evaded or never mentioned the itching and was never asked about it. She acted like a perfectly normal elderly woman, which is why she passed several psychological evaluations easily. She even chatted with the staff afterwards. We were stunned.

The next family meeting was a genuine emergency because the motel told Mom that public nudity was *not allowed* on the premises, and told her to leave if she could not keep her clothes on. Naturally she defied them. So they put her photo at the front desk to inform the clerks to reject her room reservation.

It was embarrassing. We knew that this saga would repeat everywhere.
So there was nowhere else our mother could stay for more than a day or two at best. No one dared to offer to let Mom live with them, not even for a few hours.

I could hear that she kept scratching herself, maybe as a way to ignore their comments.

There were no real suggestions, so they all defaulted to making jokes of the whole mess. I was just as perplexed.
Before any of us had a chance to think seriously of what to do, Mom announced "I can live with June! She can take care of me because she works from home!"

Mom's announcement shocked everyone, including me. So there was an awkward silence for a long time.

For me, it was alarming that Mom had suddenly changed her mind about living with us in Florida. Our secluded home in the woods was the opposite of her bustling, eccentric, city existence that offered her so much freedom to move around when she wanted to.
She would probably go insane just from the boredom of living here.
And even though her decision to stay with me was flattering, it made me nervous.

I could think of no practical reason why she would suddenly want to spend time with *me*. It would be an unprecedented event, I was sad to admit.

The only advantage to her coming here was that we had a bounty of exotic plants, which she had always wanted to cultivate but could not naturally do up north.

It was still very odd, but not threatening.

After I thought a bit more, I realized that the timing was good because my husband Edward was soon leaving for an extended trip to China for business. She could keep me company while he was gone. It could even be fun to catch up after so many years of ... kind of... not talking much.

She was right that because I worked from home, I could keep an eye on her. I could schedule time to take her shopping, or whatever, when she needed it.

The plan seemed doable.

Yet, her 'decision' still provoked an odd uneasiness in me for other reasons that I could not define.

I knew they were waiting for a reply from me. I paused again anyway before agreeing, to think if there was something I was missing.

I couldn't remember why I did not think about my mother anymore, not like I used to.

Of course, my own life got crowded over the years, as is common. Yet, I did keep in touch with a few of my siblings.

I thought it might be due to the forty-year age difference between Mom and me. That didn't seem right because Mom had always been so young in spirit, I never thought of her as old. Even as a kid, it seemed like she and I would think alike, most of the time.

I recalled that she used to playfully call me her 'last good little helper'. That was because I was the last girl at home to help, when all my sisters had gone off to get jobs and go to college.

It was fun canning vegetables and baking bread together.

That was the good-natured, practical Mother I remembered and it was practically the opposite of how my siblings saw her.

Then I suddenly felt pain at the thought of her situation. She was old, going nuts, and none of her children could care for her.

That's when I knew that I would have to help her. Under the circumstances, I knew Edward would not mind if we let her live with us for a little while. So, as they were all loud with both protests and comical banter, I coughed into the phone to get their attention.

"It's okay." I said as I imagined myself being as tiny as the phone that was delivering my words. "Its warm here and she can stay with us, at least until she gets better. She can have the guest room. There is no one else here to see her naked. Edward is going away for a while on his trip."

There was silence as everyone let my words sink in. They obviously did not expect agreement from me.

"Uh, June bug," I heard Madeline say. "You with Mom is kind of like letting a chipmunk take care of a cobra. Guess which one of you is the cobra."

They all laughed, of course, which I expected. Yet I was genuinely surprised at their lack of confidence in my ability to deal with our mother. I guess I didn't understand my older siblings all that well.

Madeline and my other sisters still perceived me as a *very* sheltered baby and kind of odd.
They weren't being mean, they were right. When we were growing up, I stayed home a lot more than they did, and not just because I was much younger. It was because I had a goofy imagination, which made me more willing to help Mom with her weird jobs. This was probably why I also

never got as offended by Mom as they did. I knew Mom had a knack for being painfully offensive, especially in the last 10 years. As we all got older she gave us self-help books, which she got from India, with badly translated titles like, 'The Swami's Recipe for Chubby Females' or 'The Childless Woman's Guide to Being Normal.'

Most of these gifts were not even applicable, but were insulting anyway, even if she meant well.

I felt confident that I understood our mother better than anyone. It seemed like I always had.

My thoughts were interrupted by Mike's harsh words. "Florida?" He blasted to Mom, "You think your *crazy* will disappear in Florida? You can fool the doctors, Ma, and maybe June for a little while, but *we* all know you are so nuts you belong in a mental institution!"

I heard Paul step in with a calmer tone. He agreed with Mike and stated, "No one here is going to enable you anymore Ma".

She snapped back, "I don't want to live in your oppressive infested homes anyway!"

Her snotty attitude was inflammatory, but Paul wisely resisted giving in to anger. He stated plainly, "June is the only one of us left who doesn't know you, Ma. When she finds out…"

"She knows me well enough." Mom sneered.

Her words both cut and comforted me at the same time. It was a weird sensation.

Paul tried to talk her out of staying with me, but Mom was determined.

She even laughed confidently. "You're all jealous because June Marie is still loyal to me."

Those simple words made my eyes fill with tears. It was true. I was deeply loyal to her simply because she was my mother. I became more determined than ever to help her find the source of the itch and then get rid of it forever.

Then I heard some mumbling until Paul announced, "Okay Mom, if you want to make this work, you'll need our help to get to Florida. So you have to agree to some rules."

She readily agreed and I wanted to hug her through the phone. I wanted to show my support by confirming to everyone that she would be just fine here with me. I wanted to tell them I was even looking forward to it, but they weren't listening to me anymore.

With the new plan and a sense of direction, all joking subsided as they mobilized for action.
I listened to a jumble of different conversations. Some were debating the rules and insisted that Mom needed drugs. Some were planning the evacuation of her Hank's Village apartment, which still had to be done.
And someone was on a phone asking about airfares to Florida for the *next day*.

That one was sobering. My gushy emotions evaporated. Reality dominated my thoughts.

Twenty four hours later Mom landed in my living room.

Part 2

Chapter 3
The First Descent

Mom's confidence was shaken severely on the airplane where she said she could feel her skin being eaten alive at 10,000 feet.

She was sweating profusely when it landed. Edward said he didn't recognize her.

When they arrived at our home, I felt a strange foreboding. I couldn't recall the last time I saw her, but the change in her appearance was drastic.

She looked wickedly old. Her severe hunch made her head hang down which made her face partly obscured. Still I could see that she was pale white except for big red blotches. Her eyes were haunting, wild, and wide, as if she knew something was stalking her.

That's when it occurred to me that a possible reason for her choosing to stay with me was so she could *die* in *my house*.

I didn't show it, but the thought of being so close to death was freaking me out. I didn't want to let her in the house. And I tried to come up with a good reason for changing my mind, other than to thwart her death plan.

Then I remembered that the doctors said she had nothing fatal. It took a moment but I chose to believe them and not my own eyes. I accepted that she just *looked* like she was dying from some horrible disease.

I took a deep breath, smiled, and gave her a hug hello.

She recoiled at my touch so I pulled away, hurt at such an abrupt rejection. I let her walk inside without any help.

She nervously scanned the house like it was a war zone of hidden enemies.

I felt pity for her fears. Then compassion crowded out my previous hurt as I pointed at the cot

I made up especially for her.

I thought she would be pleased that I chose a cot because they could not harbor skin and critters like regular mattresses could.

She didn't look pleased, but she did sit on the cot, which was as much praise as I got for my effort.

Sight of the carpet made her scowl as she then pulled her feet up to safety.

Within minutes she began itching and said she needed to use the bathroom. I moved fast to help her, thinking she needed to empty her bowels.

I was surprised that she bypassed the commode, headed straight for the shower, and stripped down instantly.

She really only needed to rid herself of the hated garments.

As she stood there naked, she slowly peered behind her to look at me, like she wanted to see my look of disgust at her hideous sore riddled body.

Of course I was too polite to show any emotion and she turned back.

However I was shocked and repulsed to see the extent of the sores. No one mentioned this.

Then I wondered if the doctors were wrong after all, and that whatever she had was actually contagious.

Panic gripped me again and my mind raced with onerous thoughts.

'Was it possible that the doctors misdiagnosed something that looked like leprosy? Was I exposed now? Would we both be quarantined? Would I have to go live in a leper colony *with her*?'

As fear reduced me to a whimpering coward, I let out a deep sob, which caught her attention.

That's when I caught the smirk on her face and my panic vanished instantly.

I impulsively decided to take a picture of the sores. I was not sure why that was so important. I guess I wanted proof of what I was witnessing. That seemed to be my habit.

I pulled out my phone and took a picture of her back where the sores were the most severe.

She heard the click and looked to see what I was doing.

To my surprise I heard myself explaining that making her better was my mission. I needed to document her progress. She accepted that explanation and even smiled with what looked to me like relief.

As happened years ago when I took care of my own sick kids, my maternal instincts kicked in.

I had to treat her, for the moment, like she was a child. I proceeded to smear aloe gel all over my mother's wretched body as if she were a baby. She didn't mind my touch as long as there was gel to separate us.

I helped her get into bed with only a light sheet as a garment. She was cooperative and I imagined that a good night sleep would follow.

Ninety minutes later she was howling in the bathroom desperate for help.

I jumped up and rushed to her, expecting the worst.

She was not hurt in any way. She had taken another shower and only needed more aloe applied. I grumbled as I applied the aloe for a second time in two hours.

I recalled what my siblings said about Mom's demand for hourly Olive oil sponge baths.

Thankfully we had no Olive oil.

That scenario became the routine for a whole week of nights.

The days were not much better, though I did observe that the itching followed a cycle, flaring up every two hours and lasting about fifteen minutes per episode.

This knowledge was little comfort since I sensed that I had no real power over her.

I let her wear a flimsy, skin baring, toga around the house and be entirely naked when in our sunny atrium. She looked like a movie alien.

To my annoyance, I started to feel so empathetic for her that I felt 'itchy' too. I resisted scratching the phantom itch, but it was very difficult.

Without enough sleep or food, I had become a neurotic drone that mindlessly got up to help her whenever she had an 'episode'.

Then one dreary night evidence of hope suddenly appeared.

As I slathered gel I realized that some of her back sores had *faded*. There was just a white scar where the ugly red sore had been. I was so thrilled I laughed joyfully and loudly.

I quickly shared the news with her, and waited for her warm praise for my good work.

Rather than be relieved, she was skeptical.

I foolishly attempted to convince her. I even took a picture which, when viewed next to the previous one, showed obvious improvement.

Yet she was still unwilling to believe the critters were gone, 'just like that'.

I let the matter rest, but was still elated as I went to sleep.

Two hours later, she was howling for help again, per the routine.

As usual I dragged my weary body out of bed to help, but I was in no rush.

The sores were fading. I even felt a tinge of pride that I had learned to adapt to the routine that would soon expire. It was like I passed a test or

won a race. I could see that the end of this grueling ordeal was not far off.
It was with this confidence that I was ready to spread the aloe and survey her back.

Then I started to shake. Anger and confusion coursed through me and I sobbed angrily. "What did you do? And *why* did you do that?!"
Instead of improvement I found dozens of new bloody, vicious, scratches crisscrossing her back.
It looked like she did this deliberately. It was worse than when we started.
She hung her head as if in shame but unwilling to confess her reasons.
Yet, if she didn't tell me, then I could not help her. She might die and I would be responsible for it.
I had to learn her motives without her confession, which seemed impossible.

However, I discerned long ago that the main reason I was so odd was because my imagination had developed into a vivid and accurate sense of empathy.

At first it was a game for me. When it became mostly involuntary, like when a chameleon changes colors, I came to dread it. I found out that getting inside the head of anyone that got too close to me was risky and often very disturbing. So I suppressed that habit.

Yet with her case, it seemed that I had no other choice. Since she was my mother, I thought she would be safe and easy to get mentally in and out of.

So, just as an actress immerses herself in a character, I let go of myself and completely cleared my mind. I let Mom's perceptions replace my own. Her descriptions of things made her world quite vivid to me. I even assumed that all her beliefs were my own, no matter how crazy they might have otherwise seemed to me.

After all that transformation, it was easy to see her world as a dark plaid landscape of prickly brambles. I noticed that everything was moving with a mass of crawling white mites. She could not move fast enough to get away from the steady stream of critters. Only scratching her skin *off* seemed to satiate them. It was her skin cells they wanted. It seemed to be a fatal solution.

I moved closer to them, to see the source of their flow. I thought I could turn it off or plug it up.

My head pounded when I sensed I was too late.

I tried to ignore the little imaginary beasts as they crawled in the fabric I was standing on, but they seemed too real. I felt the itch on my ankles. I kicked them off, convinced that they were crawling all over me. The itching got so bad I knew I had to get out. I had to retreat.

Yet leaving someone's mind is rarely complete. The perspectives I gained from empathy just accumulated in my mind like ghosts. Some were weak, and some were strong. They all haunted me, as I knew hers would.

So I strived to quickly displace her thoughts with my own. It was futile. Hers dominated and crushed mine as if I didn't even exist. It felt like the mites had reached my nose and I could not breathe. I was desperate for escape from her world. I suddenly cried out, "Stop it!"

She was startled out of her self-pity but stayed silent.

I persisted, "Stop this madness, Mother!"

She shrugged her shoulders. I was not giving up. I knew she was in control of this. For some deranged reason, she was creating the critters in her mind, and she had to stop it.

I pleaded with her saying, "Don't you know that, *for someone like me,* caring for you means that I have to *feel* what you're feeling?"

She finally said one word, "So?"

"So?" I sobbed, "So… I need *you* to *feel* better or I will *die* from this crazy itch of yours!"

She did not respond. I scratched as I sobbed, "Then I will be of no use to you, Mother!"

My begging had some effect because she stopped scratching.

Instead, she was watching me as if I was a freak show. She looked disdainful of me, like she thought me a pitiful daughter for sitting crying on the floor like a baby.

Then she turned away as she put more aloe on her arms, and said, "So I guess we'll both die from this itch of mine."

It was too cold of a response, and I eventually walked out feeling broken and alone.

Chapter 4
A Vicious Streak of Crazy

After that awful 8th night it was obvious that I needed to revise my perception of my mother.
I also needed to somehow disable my chronic, debilitating empathy.

To that end, I decided to perceive that her itching and cold aloofness were not really in her control like I thought.
I had to believe that she had some undiscovered illness which had itching and rudeness as symptoms. I became more determined than ever to find out which illness it was.

The first thing I noted was that even though the sores were definitely fading, she still scratched frequently. I insisted she get regular manicures to prevent those wicked scratches.
She still used gallons of aloe, piles of her medicinal 'Neem' leaves, which Christian sent, and the constant change of clothes.

She would not sleep in the same bed two nights in a row. She tried to sleep in the bathtub, and sometimes sitting up on the toilet. I viewed all of these as symptoms.

I took her to more doctors, to do more tests, and to get an expert explanation for the disappearing sores.

That's when I witnessed first hand how charming she could be to the gullible doctors. They failed to ask the right questions because she was sharp enough to give answers they wanted to hear. She had them completely fooled.

However they did confirm that the sores were clearing up because she was being deprived of soy, which she had a severe allergy to. This annoyed her greatly.

I soon learned that Mom did not like that I had the power to deprive her of anything.

She schemed to get the soy when I was not looking, and grew more cantankerous and even 'itchy' when she got caught with it.

It was an exhausting battle, especially when she lost. She said she was 'dying' so often that I started to believe that it might really be her last night on earth.

Finally I resorted to drugs.

Madeline had informed me that an anti-anxiety prescription was one thing Mom agreed to as part of the deal, but only if I needed them.

The pharmacist seemed familiar with my kind of sleepless face as he rushed the prescription for sleep and anti-anxiety pills.

It seemed so unfair that they were not for me.

She reluctantly agreed to take them.

The drugs brought relief, but also new and terrible problems.

As a lifelong believer in natural plant remedies she had never taken anything stronger than an aspirin.

Even in tiny doses the new drugs made her sleep most of the day. When she was awake she was mostly dizzy. Whenever that subsided, the itching returned. This rollercoaster of symptoms was exhausting to deal with, and made me feel terrible.

When I saw that she struggled simply to keep her balance while scratching, I decided to make a safe place where she did not need to get up at all for awhile.

I set up the atrium to be a kind of open air bedroom where she rested under the gentle touch of the sunlight. The sores completely vanished. The itching diminished here too. I decreased the anxiety drugs and her dizziness lessened. Even though she still woke up several times in the night and had some bouts of itching, I believed she was improving.

Then I made a mistake.

I had done some research on itching. The mistake was to *share with her* what I discovered. I explained how she might have a condition where her stressed nerves falsely trigger the release of chemicals when there was no invader, and that is what made her itch. I said it was a phantom sensation that she should ignore.

It would fade completely as her system adapted to the absence of soy. In short, the itching could actually be in her head.

She stared at me blankly as if she did not understand.

But she understood.

Her response forced me to admit her problem was more than just a physical illness.

She had a vicious streak of crazy.

It seemed that it was this irrational part of her that hated progress and anything logical, like the idea of overactive nerves and soy induced sores.

In her mind, the itching was a real itch and probably caused by the baking soda I put in with the laundry soap. This led her to believe that the baking soda brought the critters back, or that they had never left, and she panicked.

She scratched herself bloody again, even with shortened nails.

I cried at the realization that I had to increase dose of the anxiety drug again.

It was a disaster, worse than before. Even the atrium harbored enemies.

It was futile to explain anything to the crazy woman who was in charge of my mother's body.

All I could do was to make her as comfortable as possible wherever she agreed was safe from infestation.

So I prepped a new bed in the last 'safe' spot of our kitchen.

Of course, after a few hours, she did not trust that spot, and she tried to walk away, despite her dizziness. She lost her balance.

She sort of crumpled down, onto our hard porcelain tile, in slow motion it seemed to me.

She was spread out on the floor like a spoiled child waiting for attention. I was reluctant to indulge her so she howled that she had broken her hip.

My siblings warned me about how many times she had been taken to emergency rooms before, with the same complaint. Yet, her bones were still very strong, despite her age. She didn't even have a real hunch. I had recently seen her stand up perfectly straightly, with no pain, when she needed to.

I didn't understand how she benefitted from acting like she was dying.

It seemed silly to believe her. I thought she was just embarrassed that she had fallen.

Still, I felt around her leg for the break. When she did not flinch in the appropriate places, I stopped looking, satisfied that she was okay.

Predictably she howled her cry of near death.

"You're not an expert!" she yelled. "You can't know when a bone is really broken. I want a real doctor! Call an ambulance!"

Her demands were frustrating, and I was so tired of her childish games. The fact that she sought support and comfort from the people that, for so many years, she manipulated or just rejected felt mean and spiteful. It seemed like she wanted only what she thought I did *not* want.

We ended up calling the ambulance and they took her away to the behemoth hospital and, after more than 24 hours, the doctors finally found a small fracture.

Mom said that the doctors insisted that immediate hip surgery was the only thing keeping her from dying a slow painful death.

She agreed to let them put some titanium pins into her bones.

Chapter 5
The (Not So) Little Bette

Breaking Mom's hip was good for me because the post-op rehab meant I got some decent sleep for the first time in three weeks. It felt like three months.

I also found it much easier to be cheery to someone if I didn't have to be with them 24 hours a day.

She seemed to like the separation too. She looked better, even pretty, like she used to be.

At the rehab social 'mixers', she always got the most attention from the few old men who could attend. I laughed to see that she flirted with them shamelessly, like a teenager.

My only concern was that she was eating too much sweet stuff and her skin was getting 'puffy'. She had stopped eating sugar years before because she said it made her fat.

I was worried only that the itching might return again. Knowing that there would be little the rehab kitchen could offer that was soy and sugar free, I brought her food from home.

She loved my 'doting' and boasted to the nurses that she was blessed to have such a devoted daughter, and everyone agreed.

It made me feel like a kid again and I was pleased that I could help.

Strangely though, after two weeks, she called me at 2:00 a.m. all weepy and nervous to say she was dying. "I'm sure I'm going to die." she whispered frantically into the phone. "The nurses can't help me, only you can. So I need *you* to come right away to get me."

"Why me ?" I asked groggily.

She pleaded. "Because you are *the only one* who can help me find out what's wrong!"

Naturally I didn't believe she was dying or that I was the *only one* who could help her. Yet I was curious about

what was triggering the new panic. I said feebly, "I'll get there as soon as I get something to eat."
Surprisingly she accepted that, "Alright," she said. "I'll just wait for you then."
Of course, I went right back to sleep for a few hours but I did go to visit her early that day.
She looked miserable and wouldn't explain why.
So I took her for a long walk in the wheelchair around the sunny, flower-filled grounds. She gradually got better, but I had to coax her with endless amusing stories and I had to pick every flower she saw so she could 'study it for medicinal purposes'.

Finally I noticed that what really got her animated and talking was when I asked her questions about herself.
This was a relief because I was running out of stories and knew I would eventually get yelled at for stripping the landscaping of flowers.

I decided then that she was just getting bored at rehab. Yet, I liked and even needed someone else to take care of her.

To keep her mind occupied and in rehab, I encouraged her to talk about her childhood.

"I think you should write your biography." I said sincerely.

"Oh that would be lovely!" she beamed. "And you could take notes like you used to! And then you could put it all together in a booklet!"

I was a little annoyed because it wasn't what I meant, but I was surprised she remembered that I kept journals. I also hesitated to make such a commitment. Writing a biography can be a long, dark journey.

Then I thought she probably wouldn't have that much to say, and I agreed to get working on it as soon as I had time. I told her to record her stories whenever she remembered them. I'd transcribe it all later. She was thrilled and got started on it right away.

She was not going to let me forget the promise.

From then on, every walk I took with her in rehab included her telling about another part of her youth.

"Yes, Mother." I answered her question before she asked. "I will write down all that you say. I always do. You just talk, I'll listen."

When she was sure I was going to remember, she rushed back to her past.

"The chocolates were ruined!" she lamented as if the event from her childhood had just happened.

"Why?" I asked with guarded amusement.

"Because that stupid 'girl' put the moth balls in the cedar chest!"

"So?" I asked, wondering what 'girl' she was talking about.

She lamented, "That chest was hiding the box of Christmas chocolates Pa had gotten for the family!"

Since she never stated what 'girl' she was talking about, I had to ask a lot of questions. I eventually managed to extract the surprising explanation that from the time she was born in 1926 until well into her teens, her family always had a few hired servants.

"Why did you need a hired girl?" I asked naively.

She looked at me with a frown and said, "You are just like Nick. He asked me the same thing when we got married."

"You had a maid when you got married?" I asked incredulously.

"No!" she quipped. "He wouldn't let me! So I had to have kids!" She laughed heartily, which made me frown. She caught my look and turned away abruptly.

I asked, "Are you serious?"

She looked back at me sheepishly and said, "No, of course not. I loved each and every one of my darling girls."

I playfully said, "Yeah, I'd exclude those rotten boys too. They made such awful messes."

Her face got red and I guessed I had embarrassed her, though I wasn't sure

52

why. I got back to the topic. "What were you going to say about the hired girl?"

She promptly stated, "We *had* to let the hired help live with us on the farm. They got paid to cook and clean and do whatever else needed to be done. That's how it was in those days."

I was skeptical and asked, "Did you know anyone else who had servants, or who even had the room to house them?"

"No, but Pa knew how to make good deals," She stated emphatically. "He and Ma made a working farm out of a small abandoned hotel. There was plenty of room, and the servants didn't get paid too much. No one needed much back then. It was 'the Depression'. They were happy to have a roof over their head."

I tried to understand the scenario she described.

I recalled photos of her childhood home, which I always thought was rather grand for a working farm family who was not rich.

I had to admit her explanation seemed plausible even if it was rare. It was not shameful yet she seemed embarrassed about having servants.

Of course it was not how I ever imagined her because she always presented herself as a 'poor champion of the poor'. She had disdainfully intimated that servants were for those who had come from old money or royalty. I was strangely indifferent about the matter.

Before I could reassure her, she had moved on to her next fond memory. Her first dress was a lovely dusty pink plaid. She talked about the New York style dress shop she loved to shop at. She claimed she saved her own money to buy what she wanted, nothing faddish.

She was so lost in her reverie I didn't ask any questions. I just let her talk until she got to the subject of hair.

"When I was nine or ten we had a neighbor lady who was trying to be a hair stylist. I used to have a full head of wavy, auburn hair then."

She paused as she touched her slight gray curls before continuing. "Pauline loved to practice on my hair but nearly every attempt was just awful! My hair would always come out in one big frizz. Pauline said the problem was that I didn't need a permanent because my hair was already perfectly wavy. But I finally decided that I would only let a real hair stylist do my hair."

"When you were ten?" I suddenly laughed.

"No!" she was jovial, "When I was thirteen."

Then her face went suddenly sad.

"What is it?" I asked with concern.

"When I was thirteen," she began slowly, "My brother Luke died and I did it."

I was at first very alarmed at her confession. I picked a few flowers first, just to hide my emotions from her. She was happy to get the pink fragrant roses.

55

Finally I asked, "What did you mean Mother, by saying you killed your brother?

She twisted her fingers through the flowers for awhile before she finally talked.

"Luke was very gentle, kind, and thoughtful." She stated with an affectionate tone. "He wanted to be a writer, not a farmer like my other brothers. He was so helpful."

Even though I knew she had probably suffered trauma at the loss of her brother, it didn't sound like she caused his death. I thought she was just being overly dramatic.

Still, I knew she wanted to talk about it, so I obliged her by asking the appropriate questions.

"Were you very close?" I asked.

She quickly responded, "He was six years older but he always had time for me."

I asked if he was really that busy from writing.

"No," she laughed. "I mean Luke did everything for me. My folks would not let me go to town with the 'big kids' to see a movie or a concert unless Luke promised to look after me. He always did."

I casually said that I was skeptical that a teenage boy didn't care about having to babysit his little sister.

She leaned over to me and whispered modestly "I was big for my age. I was one of those girls who 'developed early'. When I was eleven, I looked just as old as my sister Mary, when she was fifteen. None of the boys thought I was a baby."

I recalled old photos of her shapeliness and knew she was right. In fact my sisters and I suffered from the same 'problem'.

But I was getting more curious about Luke. I asked casually, trying to be sensitive, "So what happened?"

She looked down at her hands for so long it seemed she didn't want to talk about it, so I started to get up.

Finally she said, "Ma and Pa liked to go on day trips. When we were all small we all went together. But by the time I was thirteen, there wasn't enough room in one car. As I said, I was big for my age. So, on Memorial Day weekend they went by themselves. They left Joe and … Luke in charge."

She was quiet again. I tried to be patient but it was getting late. "So, that was it?" I asked. "Or did your brothers have a fight or something?"

"No," she replied, "But Ma did not have a good time so they returned early Monday morning. She was very nervous. I remember seeing her checking things, looking in the barn, and the well. It was flooded. That wasn't too strange since it happens after most big storms. Still, I remember that I felt out of sorts too. We all agreed that it was unusually warm for the last weekend in May, especially for that part of Wisconsin. In fact it was so hot that we all asked if we could go swim in the Mill pond near town."

She stopped again for a long time and I was getting bored. I could see where it was going as soon as she mentioned the mill pond. Rivers and millponds were *frequent* causes of drowning, especially in rural areas. Yet, I was sensitive and asked, "So did you go swimming?"

She continued with her dramatic pauses and expressions. "It was a beautiful cloudless day but Ma was very reluctant and said 'no' to the little kids. She couldn't say 'no' to the rest of us. We were bigger than she was and could swim very well. I didn't really need looking after but she begged…"
She didn't finish the sentence so I pressed her for it rather than wait an eternity for her to get to it.
"Grandma begged what?" I asked.
She looked at me sideways and then said, "Ma begged Luke to keep an eye on me."
"That's it?" I was so impatient, and growing more annoyed with my Grandmother for being so paranoid.

59

I asked, "If you were as big as they were why did you need looking after?"

"I don't know," she replied vaguely. "Maybe it was because I was the youngest of the group."

She was quiet again and I was sure I'd have to end the drama prematurely because we'd be there forever if I didn't.

Then she spoke, "So Luke kissed her goodbye, took my hand, and we walked to the pond."

I could see she wasn't going to finish any time soon, so I reluctantly settled down and waited as she talked.

"Luke and I were ahead of the others and so we jumped in first.

Joe, Ronny and Mary were not far behind. After I jumped in I knew right away that there was a stronger current than I had ever felt before. It quickly carried me far enough from the shore that I could not feel the bottom! I thought that the storm must have washed away the sand and made the pond doubly deep."

"Yes, Mother," I said with renewed patience because she was getting so sad. "That happens sometimes."

She took my hand and continued with great emotion, "I couldn't keep my head up. Oh I know I was being silly but I was afraid I was going to drown!" She looked away in silence.

"And that's when you called for Luke to help?" I asked sincerely.

"I could see he was just about ten feet from me," she replied. "But he looked afraid too. I could see he was struggling like I was, but I yelled for help anyway."

She paused and I could see tears welling up in her eyes. I stayed quiet. She continued, "I should have called to Joe or even Ronny! They were closer! They could swim just as well. They were much bigger and stronger than Luke. *Even I was bigger* than Luke by then!"

I immediately recognized that statement as inconsistent with her story. Unless Grandma was a moron, it would have been silly to have Luke look out for someone who was bigger than himself and who could swim. I was about to correct her, but dismissed it as more dramatic exaggeration and continued to listen.

"But Luke was the one who took care of me!" She cried as if defending herself all over again. I nodded confirmation as she continued.

"Well, he must have gotten close enough to touch me, but by then, my head was under the water and I could not see him! What's worse, I thought I saw a tree branch floating right at me! When I felt something heavy on my leg, I was sure it was part of that branch and that I was going to get tangled up in it! So I kicked it as hard as I could away from me and swam back to shore on my own."

She was very upset. I touched her arm and said softly, "Maybe you were right

and it was a branch."
She wasn't listening. She continued with the sorry event. "When I crawled onto the bank I sat shivering for some time before I looked around for Luke. Joe and Ronny were wading in carefully looking for him. I suppose the log might have been Luke. But that made me more afraid! Luke would probably tell Pa and Ma that I had kicked him and then they would holler at me and probably not let me swim anymore. For a brief second I hoped they didn't find him. Then I went home by myself. I was cold. Several hours later a deputy sheriff found Luke's body well down stream."

She paused and I could see in her face that she was reliving the awful moment. I waited for her to either stop or continue. I had heard enough. She wasn't finished though.

"Luke was only eighteen years old." She stated distantly. "The whole town came to his funeral. I did not cry much, not at first. For the whole summer I didn't know how to cry. I stayed quiet. I started high school that fall. I believed everyone knew it was my fault."

I squeezed her hand mostly to keep from feeling her pain. My empathy was hard to repress.

She hardly noticed my touch and continued, "That's when I cried. I cried on my walk to school and home from school. I cried in the library. I cried during science class and during lunch. I was so wrangled by a deep sadness that I could not get away from. Nothing helped."

Then she was so quiet, I thought she had fallen asleep which was a relief. Mentally, I couldn't endure this much grief. I needed to change the subject.

I cringed when she opened her tear filled eyes and looked up at me so sadly it was unbearable.

I scrambled for a suitable exit from grief. "What happened to change that?" I quickly asked.

She seemed reluctant to leave that sorrowful place in her mind, but with some coaxing she finally said quietly, "After I fell off from seeing Clarence, I met Nick."

Chapter 6
Bette in Love

On a later walk, I got around to asking her about how she met Nick.

"Were you popular with the boys?" I asked playfully.

"Oh I don't know." she said modestly. "I could never see myself with any of the usual farm boys. Clarence was the only man I ever spent time with then."

"Who was Clarence?" I asked grateful for the opportunity to talk about something cheerful.

"I had known him for some time because he owned the radio store in town." She replied casually. "He was considerably older than I was but he was nice. When I turned eighteen he started to give me nice gifts."

"Like what?" I was intrigued.

"Oh I don't know, a brooch and some hair pins" she wavered.

"When I turned twenty he gave me a watch. He wanted me to have something that would make me think of him all the time."

"That sounds like he was serious!" I exclaimed. "How long did you see him?"

"I didn't go with him!" she balked. "I saw him once in awhile and went to a few dances with him."

"But you didn't really like him?" I asked.

"Oh he was fun, but an 'old uncle' kind of fun."

She rushed through to say, "Maybe I thought I was too old already. In those days girls could get married at sixteen if they wanted to."

"Well if this Clarence guy was rich and obviously in love with you why didn't you just marry him then?" I was perplexed.

"At that time I felt there was no one I wanted to be with." She replied. "I started thinking about joining the convent as penance."

"Penance for what?" I tried to recall what she might have meant.

She didn't answer right away. I looked at her and noticed she was twisting her fingers again.

It seemed like she didn't hear me, so I let it go. Then she continued, "I thought I should be a reverend mother and help the sickly."

I couldn't resist laughing about the irony of her becoming a mother of fourteen instead of a nun. I playfully insisted that she explain the drastic change of heart.

"Well I went to a barn dance one day." She started. "I was watching everyone else having a good time when I happened to see a foot mid way up the barn door. It was just floating there unattached to a body, or so it seemed. I laughed and went to investigate and found that the foot was attached to a handsome man with ears that were way too big for his head!"

"Dad?" I asked mostly sure.

"Of course!" She snapped happily. "Nick took my hand and we danced immediately. He was a very good dancer. We had a marvelous time! It was very romantic, except when he had to go out to the car every once in awhile to coax his brother Victor to come in and join the fun."

"Why didn't Victor want to come in?" I asked.

"Oh it turns out Vic was always sulking about something, usually girls. It's a good thing that I met Nick first. Vic was a real looker and always had girls wanting to be with him."

I asked playfully, "Do you wish that you *had* met Uncle Victor first?"

"Oh no!" she exclaimed. "Victor was too much work! He expected all the girls to *serve him*!"

I was curious about that statement and asked, "Could you explain that?"

She looked confused and replied, "Oh you know what I mean."

"No mother I don't know what you mean." I laughed. "That's why I asked."

"Well it was nicer to be his sister than his girl. That's the way it was with all of Nick's brothers."

It wasn't a good answer but I let it go and instead asked, "Do you think he liked you?"

"I suppose Victor was fond of me." She replied vaguely. "But he was fond of a lot of girls."

Then she rephrased that. "Well, he was fond of the ones he could not have. That's how Christian is. That's why he never got married."

My brother's name made me cringe. I wanted to say that the reason he never got married was because he was an ass, but I kept my lips shut.

I was very irritated that she had to brag about him *all the time*. It made me ill. I couldn't say so because she'd want me to explain why.

Thankfully I didn't have to listen to her bragging because my cell phone rang.

Unfortunately, it was him calling.

I shrugged defeat and handed her the phone.

The conversation left her very happy.

I reluctantly asked what I knew she wanted me to ask. "How is he?"

She beamed, "Christian had his first bicycle repair event yesterday and it was very successful."

"You mean he was repairing actual bicycles?" I asked doubtfully.

She frowned and said, "He shows the neighborhood kids how to repair *their* bikes. He sold a lot of bikes too."

I recalled the imaginative but terribly unsafe vehicles he liked to create. The thought made my jaw drop as I asked with surprise. "He got *paid* for one of his bikes?"

Mom scoffed at the question like I was an idiot. "He won't take money. He gave the bikes away. The kids love them!"

That actually was more plausible, and a better explanation for why he was happy about the event.

As a freakishly devout Catholic he was always on a crusade to recruit new members for the Church.

His contraptions were being used to lure in the poor, young, and aimless.

I wondered where he got the materials and asked, "How is he able to get the parts he needs to make and repair the bikes?"

She easily replied, "Well lately he's been getting a lot of it from Father Phil's junk farm. He barters for everything you know."

I was curious and skeptical and asked, "You mean he even barters for lodging and phone?"

"Yes, for that and much more." She said happily, "Christian helps

Father Phil drive his van and in return, gets to use the van to pick up and deliver junk that could be used for bikes."

I reminded her that Christian did not have a driver's license and she quipped, "Well Father Phil does, so it's okay. Besides, they are doing God's work."

That's when I stopped her from explaining any more of Christian's incomprehensible life.

Chapter 7
The First Flash of Light

One day Mom announced to us that she would be out of rehab in a week. It was only five weeks into the twelve week rehabilitation program, so I didn't believe her.

Then a few days later, I got a call from the staff coordinator. The woman did not know how my mother was able to recover from hip surgery in half the time, but the entire staff agreed my mother was finished.

The cryptic wording sounded familiar. Then I was informed that, even though she was healed, her insurance would still pay for the full twelve weeks. Unfortunately the rehab staff refused to keep her any longer.

I was not surprised that they felt my mother was a bad influence on the elderly and wanted her out immediately. However, I was annoyed that she was being released into my home. My reprieve was over.

I was embarrassed that I became so unstable at the thought of Mom staying in our house again.
So to restore my mental balance I made up a list household rules she would have to follow.

We sat out on the shady deck and I let her eat an avocado as I talked.
I thought the rules were a reasonable start.
'No sleeping outside her own room.
No night time emergencies
No aloe service.
No incontinence.
No public displays of nudity.
No more than 3 showers a day.
No cooking or fires inside the house.'

After I finished with the list of rules, I asked, "Do you understand?" she nodded without looking at me.
"Do you have any questions?" I asked.
I thought she nodded 'no' so I got up to leave.
But she then asked suddenly, "What do you do all day?"

I chose to ignore the sarcastic tone of her voice because I was flattered that she had any interest in what I did. I asked, "Do you mean what do I *write* about?"

She laughed and agreed, "Yes, that's what I meant. What do you *write* about?"

I again dismissed the faint sarcasm and replied. "I write about economics."

Her face was blank as if she was waiting for me to continue.

So I said, "I do a lot of research on the economy and then I write reviews about it. I'll never get rich from it, but it pays the bills."

Her face was still blank. I finally said, "I like to write about money."

Her face suddenly came alive and she said, "That's just like Nick! He was always worrying about money."

I felt compelled to clarify, "I *write* about money, I don't *worry* about it."

"Well he did!" she quipped as she chuckled. "He was always worrying that I spent too much money! It's a good thing you didn't finish school or he'd be hollering at you too for making him spend a fortune on that extravagant tuition!"

Her words cleared my mind of any thought.

I was silent for so long I thought I might have had a stroke. Then I realized words were coming out of my mouth.

"I did finish school mother. I went to college and got my degree."

She was quick to dismiss my accomplishment and asked, "Have you written a book about it yet?"

The simple question left me even more messed up and I had no answer. She threw down the avocado skin towards a curious squirrel and then said casually, "Nick always wanted to write a book about money which I thought strange for a chemist."

I did not know why her words hurt so badly, more than anything she had ever said before and even made me feel ashamed.

I looked down in embarrassment and she chuckled more.

She seemed to be mocking me as she kept peeling and eating her avocado until only the pit remained. Then she threw the pit to the ground and chuckled as the squirrel struggled to carry it off but was failing miserably.

I thought she was comparing me to the squirrel.

My mind had gotten so clouded that I couldn't even remember her question or what I was even doing there.

It seemed like I was upset that she found a squirrel more interesting than me. Maybe I resented the squirrel for stealing my mother's affection.

It was true I strongly disliked the pesky rodents for many reasons, but I never felt I was in competition with them for anyone's love.

So I gave up trying to understand

what had just happened and decided to take her disinterest in me as a compliment.
I wanted to believe it was her way of saying I was normal enough not to need her.

Then I suddenly got flashes of memories of how I used to help her help the needy. I even admired her for it. When I was about eleven years old she made me and the twins go with her to help feed homeless people. When she invited some of them to live with us, I tried to emulate her generosity.

But the people she chose to help had insatiable needs and were so desperate.
They even occasionally stole from us. I remembered that Dad wanted to press charges but Mom rejected that idea saying, "If they need to steal it then they need it more than we do."

After one couple stole our camper Dad was furious. He insisted the 'house guests' get screened first before she brought them home. She balked at that.

There was much tension in our house until, to Dad's relief, the problem was resolved.

Mom decided to switch to doing prison counseling which meant she could not bring the inmates home, at least not until after they completed their sentences.

I thought about how she had a habit of waiting in the places where desperate people go.

If you can see her, it means you are at the end of your hope and are in some dire need.

It occurred to me then that the squirrel and I could see her plainly.

I wondered if there was something we needed desperately.

It was obvious what the moronic squirrel needed, but I could not think of anything I was pining for.

Chapter 8
The Neem Leaf Conflict

As Mom settled into our home, I soon learned that her needs were dominating my time and caused me to neglect my work. She liked to depend on me.

Even though her walker was rapidly replacing the wheelchair, she could still not get into our shower by herself. It was not handicap accessible. She was instructed by the physical therapist to wait for me to help her.

At first I didn't mind helping, but then she started getting needy about everything. She wanted me to wait until she was finished showering. Then I had to wait until she was dressed, in case she needed help. Then I had to wait to make sure she got to the kitchen safely.

Her needs were endless. It was as if she just wanted me to be an extension of her, forever. I felt sick at the thought, especially when I realized this could continue *forever* unless we either kicked her out or we converted our shower and lots of other things in our house.

That's when I understood why my siblings would not take her. It was probably why I was so nervous about her living with us long term. Instead of just dying here, she might stay forever, wholly dependant on me.

I was so relieved that a week after getting out of rehab, Mom announced that she wanted to go to Wisconsin.

I imagined it was because she was bored with us already. Yet instead of feeling depressed and rejected by my mother I planned for her departure with some glee.

She was still mostly confined to the wheelchair but the doctors all gave approval for the trip if she did no driving. They said that a cross country drive so soon after an operation could cause blood clots. A two hour flight would be alright *if* she had assistance when she got there.

No one up there could afford to be with her for the time it would take to get her resettled. They meant that they couldn't afford it *psychologically*.

I was sorely disappointed to realize that unless *I* agreed to be her assistant then she would not be leaving.

So I decided that if she agreed to compensate me, I'd be her assistant for the time she was up there. I thought it would take about three weeks.

Unfortunately she insisted that, instead of a hotel, we should stay at the yoga center because there was a pair of cots in the meditation room that we could sleep on.

She would even pay extra for daily meditation classes for both of us.

This idea made me gag. I begged Paul to let us stay at his house because he had plenty of room, and was going to be gone much of the time.

He conceded reluctantly but only if I solemnly promised that I would *'guard his plumbing'*. I was puzzled by the strange request but readily agreed.

After a burdensome flight, we settled into Paul's pleasant bungalow on a quiet street near Lake Michigan.

A day later my siblings showed up, one by one, to say hello. They were cheery and polite. Only Christian remained unseen. Whenever odd packages were thrown at the house we knew he was there. Mom said it was his way of letting her know he was in the area, as if he couldn't just knock on the door as everyone else did.

There was no mention of the past bouts of crazy. Mom seemed very pleased at all the attention she received from her children.

However, after each visit I noticed that Mom became ravenously hungry. She began to snap at me if I suggested she wait until meal time to eat. She grew moodier and more unpredictable.

One night, we went out with Mike and his family and had a lot of fun joking about everything from family ghost stories to politics. Mom laughed a lot too. It was not a stressful evening.

Yet, minutes after getting back to Paul's, who was not there, she snapped at me saying, "Get me my Neem leaves!"

Her foul mood and tone were a complete shock to me. The Neem leaf issue was also new and perplexing.

Ever since Mom went to India where the Neem grows naturally, the Neem tree became her favorite for medicine.

Then when she came to stay with us, Christian mailed her fresh 'medicinal' leaves which he called Neem leaves.

Yet she must have known that those *fresh* leaves could not have been the leaves of the tropical Neem tree which can't grow in Wisconsin. The leaves he gave her were obviously curry leaves which look and smell nothing like Neem.

So it was bizarre and confusing that she would refer to these leaves as Neem, as if she didn't know plants.

It was also confusing that she would tell me to get them for her when they should have been easily within her reach.

I guess I hesitated too long from thinking because she snapped again, "You took my Neem leaves now you give them back!"

Her tone was so demeaning and her accusation so boggling I just stared dumbfounded until she snapped again, "These leaves are my medicine! I need my medicine or I will *die*!"

The word 'die' pulled me out of my stupor as I quickly looked around the house for the 'lost' envelope of leaves. I eventually found it right next to where she was still standing.

I immediately thought this was a sign of dementia and felt a strong wave of emotion for her. I wanted to hug her and help as much as possible.

Then she snapped me out of that sentiment with the command, "Give me my Neem leaves!"

I handed her the small package. She took it greedily without a thank you or any explanation as she closed the door behind her.

From that moment on I have hated 'Neem' leaves.

I couldn't dwell on this for long because I had to plan her visit and, most importantly, I *had* to find a place for her to live.

She did not make any of this easy. Her mood was foul and distracting. Her needs were endless.

After just 72 hours from arrival, she demanded that I look at 'the thing' on her back. I cringed of course and expected to see a return of the horrible sores.

Fortunately it was just one big pus-oozing boil. I only had to drop Epsom salt into it and change its bandages twice daily. There was no need for aloe smearing!

As I took care of the boil I asked about what she thought might have caused the spontaneous eruption. She claimed it was from plastic but I suggested that it might be due to stress, which can sometimes be the cause of boils.

"I'm not stressed!" Mom scoffed at my ignorance.

"How would you describe the way you've been lately?" I asked.

She was silent as she fidgeted with my cell phone in her hands.

I recalled the first phone conversation she had when we got off the airplane. Christian hated the 'government-subsidized' airplanes and wanted Mom to drive, not fly, to Wisconsin.

I don't know why she lied to him about it. He was not that stupid and he was furious when he found out.

Their conversations were always eccentric and this was no different.

"No! I had to fly or I could have a stroke!" she had rasped dramatically into the phone. "I can't take a car, not even if a priest is driving me! I'm not riding with Father Phil ever again because he's blind as a bat and you know it! You shouldn't be helping him drive; you don't even have a license! He'll be the death of you! No, that's not okay! A parent shouldn't outlive their children! It's a bad omen!"

Over the subsequent few days, this phone dialogue was repeated several times, and Mom was getting visibly weary from it. Christian could rant for hours on the phone for the dumbest things. She never complained to me about him. Instead of chastising him for being an ass she usually just listened and retreated into a 'happy' world where everything was 'fine'. That's what she told me, like I believed her.

I knew Christian was nuts, and that listening to him caused all kinds of stress. The boil on her back was probably caused by stress from enduring his rants and crazy logic.

Then I dimly recalled some old stresses of my own that led to things like boils.

I couldn't remember the details but didn't really want to remember.

Instead I hastily finish up the bandaging and left her alone so she could call Christian, on *my* cell phone.

Chapter 9
The Madison Trip Down

The Wisconsin trip soon revealed even darker shades of Mom's personality.

I had planned to spend *one* day with Mike's two little girls, Allie and Beth, on a day that Mom would be spending with her friends.

The girls wanted to see the state capital which they had never been to. Mom would have no interest because she had been there hundreds of times already as a chaperone for our school field trips.

So I planned the whole trip carefully for just me and the girls. I told mom where I'd be and who would be taking her around that day. She nodded in understanding, but looked sad, like I was excluding her.

I felt badly so I reminded her that it would be too difficult for me to push her around while also keeping an eye on the girls. It's a five story building. It would be boring for her to be by herself and confined to the first floor.

She nodded and replied happily. "Oh that's fine. I've been to the capital many times."

I was relieved that she understood and said "Good." and I continued to gather a few things for the trip. Then I heard that she was still talking. "It will be nice to just sit down on the first floor by myself for a change."

It took awhile for me to understand what she meant. I did not actually invite her and she knew that I had already arranged for one of her friends to pick her up later. When I realized that she expected to join us I was surprised and confused.

I reminded her that she had plans to visit her friend Carol later.

"Oh she can't make it." Mom said quickly. "I called her just a few minutes ago. She's very forgetful. She's schizophrenic you know. Besides, I can see Carol anytime."

I was skeptical that Carol was that far gone. I wondered if I should call to confirm this change of plans.

Unfortunately, Mom didn't give me the chance. In those few minutes I was thinking, she had already packed her stuff and was waiting in the car Madeline had lent me.

I suspected then that she had planned all along to go to Madison with us.

It was raining for most of the two hour drive to the capital.

I didn't think about what it would be like to bring a handicapped person along, especially if it was raining, and so had not thought to check beforehand which entrances had wheelchair ramps.

Unfortunately it was still raining when we got there and we had to push Mom all around the outside of the building to look for a ramp. We all got soggy and tired. The girls were real troopers, never complained, and even took pictures of the capital building they thought looked like a castle.

Once inside we all agreed it was worth the effort. The glittering floor of the dome was bright with gold lettering and tiles. The walls were covered with stunning paintings and gorgeous soaring murals. I was relieved that this was where I would be leaving Mom.

Then an annoying exchange occurred shortly after we entered the center rotunda.

The girls wanted to buy something to remember the day and the place. I steered them and Mom towards the information booth that was being tended by a handsome young man, Robert. I was sure we could find a good memento there.

Robert was very talkative and helpful. He told us that there was a gift store in the building that had just what we were looking for.

Satisfied with his information I started to turn Mom's chair towards the gift shop. Then, as if he had not helped us enough, Robert stated abruptly that a tour was starting in 5 minutes.

I stopped to look at the girls and gauge their interest. They were a mature eight and nine, but they were also very energetic and would want to explore freely without constraints of a tour. I didn't think they would last very long listening to an old man talk about the history of Wisconsin.

I was about to decline his offer until I saw that Mom was smiling at him and nodding yes.

Unfortunately as I was frowning at Mom, Robert was smiling at me. He mistook my frown for concern for Mom's lack of mobility in her wheel chair. Before I could stop him, he announced loudly for Mom to hear, "You can still take the tour with a wheelchair by using the elevators on each floor and rejoining the group."

I was about to explain why my mother was okay with staying on the first floor, but Mom was way ahead of me. Before I could even catch a breath she beamed at the man and said, "I would love that!"

I was instantly discouraged and annoyed, but Robert did not notice because he was pointing to the elevators.

Obligation overwhelmed me and quickly suppressed my annoyance. I noticed that the words, "Thank you." were coming from my mouth as I pushed Mom to the elevators.

As the girls, Mom, and I finally 'rejoined' the group we could plainly see that *Robert* would be our tour guide.

That was even more irritating. It seemed that Robert had just been pushing to get more people into his tour. He probably got a 'head count' bonus.

Then I saw how excited the girls were to see him. They laughed loudly at first and then to me they giggled, "He's sooooo cute!"

He heard their comments anyway and smiled sheepishly at us. They listened intently mostly because they loved getting close to him.

I was thankful that his attractiveness kept the girl's attention because it gave me a chance to maneuver Mom's chair every time the group moved.

By the 3rd floor, the infatuation the girls had for Robert faded and they were losing interest.

However, my interest in Robert increased as I saw how sharp he actually was. I wondered why he was just a tour guide. He explained in detail how it was a strategic position. I was very impressed.

We were getting along well enough for him to grant my request to let the girls sit at the governor's desk and other usually off limit activities. It was quite fun for me and the girls. Unfortunately, guilt about leaving Mom alone, even briefly, kept nagging me. Trying to satisfy everyone, including myself, was mentally and physically exhausting.

I got tired and careless, especially with my words. I said harmless flirtatious things to Robert that I should not have within earshot of Mom, who heard me.

She acted like she had caught me in something scandalous and judged me harshly for it.

"I can see why you only wanted the girls to go with you." She said quietly, and for only me to hear.

I really did not care what she thought. The group was moving again, and I was trying to keep my eye on the girls while pushing her along.

She was not finished. "Did you know you were going to see him when you planned this trip?"

I vaguely caught on that the question was loaded. It made me recall similar comments, like the typical Catholic ones I encountered as a child. There was no escape from such judgments. So I shrugged it off and simply replied truthfully and with great fatigue. "I never saw him before mother."

"You sure acted like you knew him." She scoffed.

By that time, I was tired of her whole attitude, and that last jab was not helpful. I was tempted to just walk away and let her fend for herself. She could push her own stupid chair.

Thankfully for her sake, Robert unwittingly intervened. The tour had just ended and he came to talk to us.

He got my mind off of the idea of abandoning Mom as he told me about a special speaker that evening. The topic was economics. He offered to get us in for free as his guests.

I truly wanted to attend but knew she would not like it, even if I got the girls to look after her.

I thanked him and very reluctantly declined his invitation. The girls gave him a quick hug goodbye and ran off giggling.

Mom smiled up at him flirtatiously and thanked him reverently, like he was an angel. I nearly gagged at her hypocritical display.

He politely directed us to a ramped exit, unaware of the minor drama between me and my mother.

It was still drizzling when we emerged from the maze-like Capital building. That's when I remembered that we had not bought any state capital token. I was too exhausted to push Mom around anymore, and she couldn't be left outside in the rain while we went back in. I couldn't let the girls go inside alone. My irritation was getting very hard to suppress.

Then I became aware that if I was going to push Mom anywhere I would need food. I had a bad habit of forgetting to eat. Since the girls were hungry too, we all agreed to eat first and then get a memento at the museum next door to the capital.

We drove around the block until we found something we all agreed on. I quickly parked and we rushed to the exciting crowded restaurant. I felt much better after eating, even though neither the weather nor Mom had changed.

The rain did not hinder the girls and me from wanting to explore the cool shops around the capitol. I decided that it was too rainy to bring Mom along. I assured her that our adventure could not last long and so her stay in the car would be short. Mom accepted her fate quietly as we quickly put our very last coins into the parking meter and then ran happily along the rainy sidewalks.

We got cookies first, for more energy and then made our way to the museum. The girls rushed in, gave a cheery 'hello' to the attendant, and browsed all the options. Finally they bought a snow dome and a silver statue of the capital.

"Good choices!" I smiled. "It's really pouring now, so do you want to wait until it lets up and see the rest of the museum?"

They peered mischievously out into the rain and said together, "We want to run in the rain!"

I did too but felt obligated to offer the mature and responsible choice first.

"Okay then" I said. 'Now button up your coats and be careful"!

It is delicious to run in the rain once in awhile. I felt like a giggly ten year old again.

When we ran the block down the steep street back to the car I must have forgotten about Mom. I instinctively took out the keys to unlock the door, even though she was still inside and could have unlocked the doors for us.

At that moment I caught a glimpse of Mom's frown through the glass. I suddenly felt guilty for having fun while she sat in the dampish car.

The frown instantly provoked me to look away and at the girls splashing in the raging gutters. Seeing them made me smile again.

So guilt and laughter were running through my mind simultaneously, as rain drenched my body, my hands, and the keys they contained.

I tried to hold tighter to the slippery plastic fob but the keys slipped away as easily as the rain and down into the storm drain I then realized I was standing *right on top of.*

A gaudy sick kind of feeling melted through me as I herded the girls into the car and slumped behind the steering wheel as if nothing had happened.

Mom was still oblivious but the girls were sharp for their age and sized up the predicament in seconds.

They knew we had lost the keys and we had no spare. It would be a two hour drive to bring the spare, and their dad, Mike the plumber, would be mad if he had to be the one to make the trip. And who else would come out there except their father? They knew I had to deal with all of this alone because Mom was no help.

When she finally caught on to what happened we listened to her 'too late' comments quietly.

My silence made Mom more indignant. She treated me like I had been bad and implied I deserved this for how shameful I was to Robert, the nice tour guide I had apparently corrupted.

I could not tolerate the self-righteous,

condescending tone and decided it would be better to go inside the museum to think about a solution rather than stay in the car with her.

I announced, "The girls and I will go and ask someone in the museum for help."

Mom was pleased that I was taking what she thought was her advice.

I had no intention of asking for help I thought would be of no use. Once inside I made a few phone calls to siblings but no one answered. I left messages explaining the dilemma.

The girls and I toured the museum until there was nothing more to see. Then I did ask for help, for lack of anything better to do.

An elderly man who was the volunteer handyman agreed to take his 'stick-with-wax- ball-on-the-end' to try to retrieve the keys.

I was sure it was futility because the torrent of rain on the steep sloping road would have carried the keys far off by now. I grumbled to myself about choosing absolutely the *worst* parking spot for such a rainy day.

I agreed to try the 'wax ball' only to pass the time until someone returned my call.

The girls and the old man peered down into the drain and watched intently as the wax ball brought up stones, a penny, and a magnet.

I had to admit it was an impressive device. Beth was most intent on seeing it work. The man had to keep nudging her out of the way until finally I had to ask her to step aside for a minute.

Beth stepped away and looked intently up and down the street, as if trying to decide which way was best. Then she moved down the block a bit.

I got nervous that she might wander off in the rain. Then I saw that she was standing off the sidewalk and again peering down at something.

I was about to scold her to get out of the street, but she suddenly stood up and hollered "I see the keys!"

The words were alien at first and so improbable. Yet Beth was certain and so I believed her. We all quickly ran to see what she saw.

There was another storm drain, miraculously only 15 feet away and *down stream* from the first drain. In all my years I had never seen storm drains placed this closely on the same side of a street. It was excessive and I never would have thought to look.

Yet, we could all plainly see that the keys were there, perched on the mound of pebbles at the bottom of the drain, seconds away from being carried away by the torrent of water.

The man quickly dropped his stick and easily retrieved the keys.

I held onto them tightly until they were safely in my deep pocket.

We all stared at Beth who was nonchalant about her discovery. "It was logical." she said like she was a master plumber. "The water couldn't be flowing anywhere else but down here. Steep slopes like this have more storm drains now. I just used my eyes to spot the keys. That's all."

The man said kindly that Beth had pretty keen eyes. I hugged Beth and thanked and praised her profusely.

She was cool about the whole thing and I admired her even more.

As we piled back into the car the awful sickening stress vanished as relief oozed through me.

I called everyone back and left 'problem solved' messages.

We drove in silence the rest of the way home. I had a lot of time to think.

I realized, as if it was the first time I met her, that it was a bad idea to bring Mom along because she acts like she has to dominate everything, like a queen defending her throne. Any competition is a threat, even if it's from her granddaughters. So it was futility to try to split my attentions between her and the girls.

It took me several days to recover from that confusing and strangely bad trip. Mom's chronically condescending attitude and bossiness did not help. I had to get away and take a break.

I decided to spend the morning looking for apartments for Mom. I arranged to take Madeline to work in exchange for use of her car.

I tried to evade Mom but she was sharp enough to easily guess my plans. She beat me out to the car the morning Madeline arrived.

Obviously I should have just said 'no', but felt too weak to force her removal from the car and I just didn't want to fight with her.

Madeline saw my defeated expression and gave me a sympathetic hug. She couldn't say no to Mom either.

After we dropped off Madeline and we were alone in the car, Mom began talking of all the things she needed.

She never asked for things, she just stated that she needed them. I knew I was going to get everything she stated. It seemed futile to resist or to carry out my own plans for the day. My own will seemed crushed.

As I conceded to this feeble-looking yet covertly- powerful old woman, I wondered how I got myself into such a ridiculous trap.

At first I thought that my entrapment started the moment I agreed to help find the source of her itching.

Yet it seemed that everything began somewhere in the time before the itching started.

The past was kind of murky and parts of it I had put away a long time ago. I couldn't quite recall why. I decided to think yet again about what I actually knew about my mother.

Obviously I knew all her kids, her husband, and her siblings.

I knew about her childhood, from what she told me recently.

From my own childhood I remembered that canning was nice for me and my closest brother Jack, but realized that canning only happened once a year.

Making bread with her happened a lot, but only when I was about ten.

I liked helping her.

That was it. I could not recall anything else. I knew as much about her as I would about a stranger I had just met.

Of course there had to be more to fill the gaps in my memory. I was probably just too hostile and tired to remember any at the moment.

Anger is exhausting to maintain and there seemed to be a lot of it flowing between us. It was part of the trap.

Sooner or later I'd have to say 'no' to her and I'd have to face the fight I was avoiding.

So I decided to resolve the problem maturely.

"Mom," I began timidly. "Can we talk?"

"Of course" she said cheerfully, like we were buddies.

I bit my tongue to suppress anxiety and took a deep breath.

"When people spend a lot of time together non-stop, like we have, it is normal that they start getting on each other's nerves. They start irritating each other."

"Oh yes," she nodded in agreement but not in understanding.

I pressed on. "To avoid getting mad at each other, the best solution is for the individuals involved to spend a little bit of time alone."

"Yes," she nodded again. "That can be good."

I could see she still was not following me. I continued to be polite with my words. "So, I'm feeling kind of irritated and I need some time alone. I'm not mad. I'm just overwhelmed with everything. Okay?"

"Okay," She responded sincerely. "I think I understand."

I believed that she finally did really understand and was pleasantly surprised at how well she took my request. I had a new respect for her and felt sheepish about perceiving she had trapped me somehow or that there was deep hostility between us. Then I noticed that she had more to say.

"I'm not surprised that you're so overwhelmed with all you have been doing! I think you need to take a break or you'll get sick."

It sounded like she was suggesting that I take a break from caring for her and I asked hopefully "What do you mean?"

She chatted happily, "I mean that I just want you to know that no matter what happens I will always...," she paused and patted my hand warmly, "...am always surprised that things turn out okay with what you choose to do."

I instinctively smiled and felt warm for awhile.
Then the words settled and I began to digest them. I sensed there was something missing. It seemed that the words '...no matter what happens I always...' should have been followed by something like 'will love you'.
I went over her entire sentence again in my mind and was sure that 'I love you.' was no where in her statement.
Angst was soon churning in my bowels.
I really did not want a fight but I felt I was sinking into one. I really wanted

her words to match my positive perception so I waited for her to add something actually nice. She said nothing more, and that silence burned me more than anything she said.

I should have just let it go. But instead I asked her to explain what she meant, like that would make me feel better.

"Well," she began nicely. "I thought it was a bad idea from the start for you to take me to the capital *and* the girls too. I didn't mind having the girls there but I could see that you were getting so worn out."

The anxiety of that trip flooded my mind again. I struggled to control my new bout of anger. It sounded like she was criticizing me for bringing the girls along.

I wanted to scream that she should stop acting like she's the 'queen' all the time but heard she had more to say.

"You are just working too hard." She said sweetly. "But you managed to make it work out after all."

Her tone and words suddenly sounded reasonable and my anger dissipated. I sensed that I was probably overreacting. I felt sheepish again about thinking so harshly about her so I replied with a quiet, "Thank you."

That should have ended the matter but it didn't. She felt it necessary to repeat herself with a small rewording, "I mean, it always surprises me how you can turn all the bad situations you've been in into something a little better. Your whole life you've always worked too hard."

Her words seemed like both a compliment and a kick in the gut at the same time. It was as if her urge to compliment me was in conflict with her urge to offend me.

It left me wondering if she meant that I was always in bad situations and that I only succeeded in making them *slightly* better than bad. Was she saying that I choose bad situations in the first place? Was she thinking my whole life was a failure and was she surprised I ever made it this far?

Trying to interpret her real meaning was maddening, especially because I desperately wanted her words to be a compliment. Unfortunately, the kick in her words was easier to feel than the compliment was to find. I realized that I was struggling to suppress a rage of tears. Something deeper in me was being jarred loose.

Yet I wanted to ask her to clarify what she really meant. I thought maybe I was wrong again and that there really was some praise in her words.

But something else was telling me to retreat from my mother. She had just hurt me with merely a particular combination of a few words. I was not verbally strong enough to retaliate.

In verbal battle, any question is retaliation in disguise.

So I pushed my bruised and confused emotions aside and forced myself to focus on something unrelated and hopefully safe.

My task list for the day would have to do.

Chapter 10
The Brain-Crystal Phone Battle

The first item on my task list was to buy more minutes for my prepaid phone because she was using it so much.

I couldn't recall why I let her do that except that I rarely used it.

That's when I decided that I would stop sharing my cell phone with my mother.

"Mom," I said coolly as I drove, still beleaguered from the verbal hits she inflicted moments before. "I'm getting you your own cell phone."

She recoiled as if in pain from being punched.

"I don't need a phone." she hissed.

I did not expect such a dramatic reaction and found it amusing.

Instead of matching it, I calmly responded, "Paul doesn't have a land line anymore and I can't leave you alone without a phone."

"So don't ever leave me alone." She offered feebly as if she didn't care.

I suddenly had a revelation that made it clear to me that she cared a lot. In fact, what she said was exactly what she wanted. The shared cell phone was a cord that bound me to her so she would *never* be alone. That was understandable for someone her age, but would be an extreme sacrifice for me. I dismissed her suggestion as nonsense.

She was not happy at the new arrangement. I chuckled to myself at how much of a defeat she believed she suffered just because of that stupid phone.

She brooded in silence for a long time until we got to the store where I would be buying the cursed phone.

Then she finally and loudly hissed her official reason, "Millions of monkeys are being killed for their brain crystals to make those phones!"

I truly hated the newspaper article that gave Mom the 'monkey brain-crystal' idea. Now it was in the 'fact bank' of her brain and she will never cease referring to it.

I didn't bother to explain how mathematically impractical it was to rely on monkey brains for cell phones.

She would just use my explanation as a foundation for the opposite theory and then get me to agree to research it to prove which is correct. It would be like trying to prove aliens were 'not at the first Thanksgiving'. Even thinking about it gave me a headache.

I avoided the 'research it' trap by pointing out her hypocrisy, "How are you not using monkey brains now when you use my cell phone?!

"Every time you buy *another* phone you shed the blood of yet *another* monkey which is one of God's creations too!" she retorted.

"Well" I replied quietly, not accepting her solution, "I'll say a prayer for that ape because your safety is more important to me than a monkey's brain."

She sulked in her seat as I parked and walked away.

When we got back to Paul's I showed

Mom the newly purchased phone and explained the instructions but she ignored me completely, like I did not even exist.

I finally said, "You cannot use my phone Mother. If you don't want this one I will return it and you'll have no way to contact anyone."

She still said nothing, but closed her eyes and started to pray, probably for me. I walked out fuming at her childish sulking. Cursing through my pressed lips, I trudged angrily along some path for a long time until a cliff stopped me. The view below of the vast expanse of water calmed me instantly.

After some time, the walk along the shore of Lake Michigan cleared my head. I decided that her strange cantankerous behavior towards me was just due to her old age and dementia. It was the nicest, easiest explanation that I could think of. It served to liberate me from having to understand all the possible and confusing meanings to her words.

I was sure that there would still be fights, but I didn't have to be offended by her assaults because she was just old and she didn't mean to hurt me.

I returned an hour or so later refreshed and calmer. I found her brooding out in Paul's garage where my siblings had stored some of her things.

I was surprised to see she had found the garage opener which I had deliberately hid on top of the refrigerator. I was more surprised she could actually use the fairly complicated electronic device. This fact meant I probably had to eliminate dementia as one of her symptoms.

"I want my stuff moved into the house!" she yelled belligerently as soon as she saw me.

I quietly reminded her, "You know you have to ask Paul first before anything is brought inside his house."

She snapped, "I'm the mother! I can do what I want."

I calmly responded, "Even mothers should respect their children, especially those that work so hard. There needs to be mutual respect between parents and children."

She was not happy with my impudence.

"He should respect me because I gave him life!" She barked angrily. "I gave life to all of you! You should be honoring me!"

Her response was unexpected and harsh but I didn't flinch.

I stated firmly, "Giving us life does not mean you have claim to everything we have achieved. Why can't you be grateful that your son is being so hospitable to us?"

The disdainful roll of her eyes and mocking gestures were further clues that she did not agree with me. Still, I stood my ground against her mental assault until she turned away, a few books in hand, and hobbled to the picnic table.

When I could see she was safely seated I went inside and ate a whole bag of chocolate.

I think I won the battle of the monkey brain-crystal phone, but I sensed the 'war' was not over.

Chapter 11
Neem Compromised Plumbing

The Neem leaves issue was my constant bane ever since I asked her to explain how it was possible that the tropical Neem tree could grow in Wisconsin.

Instead of admitting she was wrong, she just got more obnoxious about it. She took every chance to ask me where I put her 'Neem' leaves, like repeating it a million times would mean they were not curry.

I matched that strategy with statements like, "I have never seen fresh Neem leaves anywhere in Wisconsin, but I did see your curry leaves in the bathroom where they should not be."

This usually prompted her to assume the role of a seasoned medicine woman and scoff, "Ha! I know enough about India to know what Neem leaves look like. I was there twice."

"Good." I responded sharply. "Then you should know that what you are now sucking on are curry leaves."

She scoffed again but continued to suck on the tough, raw, caustic leaves of curry until a few blisters appeared at the corner of her mouth and made her teeth black. This was how she took her 'medicine'.

It was a silly battle. I finally caught on to how it all started.

Christian lied first that the leaves were Neem because he did not want to disappoint her with the truth. She went along with it to avoid making him feel badly about lying. She repeated the charade to me to protect his reputation. It was circuitous logic.

When I tried to stop the nonsense she continued it because she could see that the Neem/Curry thing really bothered me. It was her way of making me sore about something too, like she was about the new cell phone.

So I just stopped trying to challenge the curry. It was a truce of sorts.

Then one day I noticed a foul stench in the air like burning oil.

It was emanating from the kitchen where Mom was boiling the leathery curry leaves, apparently to soften them up.

I choked on the black smoke and insisted that Mom had to stop or Paul would have a fit and evict us.

Surprisingly, she did stop, maybe because she was choking too. I didn't hang around to see where she put the foul greens, because I needed fresh air.

Later though I noticed she had put the mass of now black muck into the kitchen sink, but not into the garbage disposal.

I never gave it a thought as I mashed the gob with a spoon down the drain.

After a week of this, I noticed the kitchen sink would not drain.

I never suspected curry leaves could be responsible because I thought they were long gone with every grind of the disposer. Even after I plunged the kitchen sink, it still would not drain and I wanted to cry.

Paul would be back soon from his trip. I could not let him know I *failed* to protect his plumbing, despite his stern warnings.

The next step was to crawl under the sink and twist off the 'clean out' cap. I was relieved that nothing poured out. That meant that the clog was above the floor, not under it. The spoon I jabbed into the drain from below disturbed a foul smelling black gob that plopped with a splash into my lap.

I was splattered, but not defeated, by the cursed leaves, many of which were still intact even after being put through the grinder.

I was pleased that I had solved the problem so I put every thing back and crawled out.

Mom was obviously waiting for me because she immediately called out, 'Get me that spoon.'

I obediently looked at the desired spoon on the drying rack, a few feet out of her reach.

Without any thought, I got up, cleaned the black gob off my hands and delivered the spoon.

It was then time to test the drain.

As I let the water fill the sink, I realized that Mom could have gotten the spoon. I wondered why she made demands for things she could easily get herself. I also wondered why I was so mindlessly programmed to serve her. I wasn't dependent on her for anything. Why was I so blindly loyal?

I pondered all of this as I watched the water seep down the drain.

It was as sluggish as the panic that was oozing through my nervous system.

I could see my dendrites flashing as the news spread that I had failed to unclog the sink.

Conflict was imminent. My whole body tensed up as if preparing for an attack.

Mom's voice instructing me to turn off the burner and get her a mango pulled me out of my trance, even though I did not respond to her.

I could see the time and knew Paul would be back any minute.

I thought briefly about Beth and how she used logic to find the keys. This was not so simple so I resorted to calling her dad, Mike because he was the plumber who could help with this.

Mom did not like being ignored, or was nervous or something, because she kept telling me to do things even when she could see I was on the phone explaining the problem to Mike. Maybe she was trying to suppress information that implicated curry leaves.

Mike was very understanding and walked me through the 'trouble shooting' steps to unclog drains.

The obstructionist complaints of Mom were distracting. She insisted it was the faulty idea of 'garbage disposals' that led to this clog.

"I told you all along that Neem leaves were never meant to be put down a drain!" she rasped. "You were just too stubborn and lazy to dig a compost pile out in the yard like I told you to do in the first place!"

Mike could hear every cutting jab Mom delivered and knew I was losing it. He also knew about Paul's plumbing phobias and the chewing out I would get for this. It had to get fixed before Paul returned.

He agreed to get there as soon as possible if I could take care of the girls while he worked on the clog.

I assured him I would and would even get Mom to pay for his time.

I hung up the phone and finally breathed.

Mom acted naive and asked with delight, "Are Mark and Mike both coming over to visit?'

"Not Mark." I said as I moved to my room to lie down because my head was pounding, praying that Mike got there before Paul did.

Unfortunately, the minute I lay down, Paul drove up.

My anxiety zoomed and I shot up to go remind Mom what not to say.

"Paul is back, Mom!" I stated, "Please do not deny anything. Don't say it was not your fault! That only gets him more pissed!"

"What isn't my fault?" she asked innocently.

"Just don't say anything." I retorted. "Don't mention the curry leaves!"

"I don't have any curry leaves" she laughed.

I cringed and waited at the sink for Paul, hoping he'd head right to his room and skip the kitchen.

No such luck. His paranoia about the plumbing was well founded when Mom was around. She apparently had a knack for this sort of thing. He took one glance in the sink and immediately recognized the telltale signs of blockage. He was no amateur.

He rapidly exploded like he used to sometimes when I was little and got him mad. "I knew this was going to happen! Why didn't you listen to me?! Why the fuck didn't you guard the damn sink?!"

I withered under his fury, and he didn't stop to let me talk. He kept roaring, "I told you not to put shit down here!"

His tirade was solidly aimed at me, the one who promised to be responsible for Mom's actions.

Yet he didn't see me as an adult who was unfairly saddled with this ridiculous situation.

In his eyes I was still the spoiled little eight-year old of his youth, eleven years behind him. I deserved to get yelled at.

Mom sat within ear shot of the scolding but did nothing as she continued to eat her mash of leaves and beans.

I knew the clog was her fault, but was reluctant to tattle. She would deflect blame with no effort and would just as easily build a case against me worse than I could imagine.

In her mind too, I was an impudent child that needed a good scolding once in awhile. My scolding was also penance for killing monkeys.

So instead of arguing or defending myself, I ran off to a quiet place to cry, just like I always did when I was in fact a child, some thirty years ago.

When I walked back to the house hours later, Paul was gone and Mike was just finishing up the elaborate repairs.
I apologized that I wasn't there to watch the girls like I said I would. He said it was 'okay'. I wrote him a check from Mom's account and asked him to talk to Paul for me.
 "Tell him I'm going to give him a break from us." I said. "Madeline said we can stay with her for the rest of the visit. No hard feelings."
Mike laughed with understanding and agreed. He also relayed the message from Paul that he was very sorry for

getting so mad and losing it. He was actually happy that the plumbing got fixed finally because it had needed those repairs for years.

I was glad Paul was not still mad.

I said "Thank you" and "Goodbye" to the girls, who gave me nice understanding hugs. They whispered, "We get yelled at too, all the time."

I smiled and waved as they pulled away.

Then I tried to put the whole sorry day behind me, but when I got back inside Mom was waiting for me.

"It was lucky the clog happened when we were here," She commented casually, "Because now he has $400 worth of new plumbing and did not have to pay for it."

The fact that she had been listening enough to know how much I paid Mike was more evidence of her still-sharp mind. This statement indicated what a shrewd woman she could be. She still firmly believed she was not at fault for the clog and she did not agree to pay for it. She wanted something in return for her $400.

She was waiting for a reply but I was so tired I couldn't think of anything rational to say. Then, to my relief, my mouth opened.

"A few weeks of accommodations in a house for one person and an assistant would cost more than $400." I stated plainly. "You got a good deal."

I looked at her sideways and watched that she actually nodded and seemed satisfied with my answer.

I did not wait for her to change her mind. I walked quickly past her to my room, closed the door, and ate more chocolate.

The remainder of the visit was more of the same and worse. Mom seemed to resent my siblings, especially my sisters. I was too mentally fatigued to figure out why. I tried hard to find a place to leave her but failed. Everything I suggested was somehow problematic for her.

Finally she said, "Why don't we stay longer so you can find a place that *you* like."

"Why would I do that?" I asked perplexed.

"Well I'll be fine wherever you are." She stated casually.

I was confused for a bit and then asked, "Are you saying you want me to find a place for us to *live together*?"

"Isn't that why you're here in Wisconsin?" she asked innocently. "What else have you been looking for? I mean, now that Edward is leaving you."

I was cut low at her perception and said quietly.

"Edward will be coming back, Mother."

She gave me a crushing look of pity and said, "I know, but it might be a good idea to look for something else anyway."

She was so condescending I wanted to smack her, but the thought of her 'solution' for Edward's leaving me was debilitating.

I whispered sadly, "So you would be okay if I gave up my life in Florida to take care of you here."

"Only if that is what you want."

She replied sweetly and with understanding. I felt suddenly sick and said, "No, Mother, it's not what I want. I want to go back home to Florida."

I did not say aloud that I really wanted to go home alone, without her.

Part 3

Chapter 12
The 3rd Ceramic

To my disappointment Mom returned home with me after all. She claimed she needed the warmth of Florida to heal.

I didn't bother to say how Wisconsin in July is still warm and she could heal just as well there.

I didn't bother to ask her to apologize for all her nastiness to me while there because I believed she was still sick.

I decided to be a good Christian who forgives and forgets. It was much easier to forgive her than confront her about it anyway.

However, I found it was not so easy to *forget* some of the things she said.

Her words still shook me every once in awhile, like someone was trying to wake me up out of a nice deep sleep. I ignored her words in order to more easily let bad memories quickly fade. It was my way of maintaining civility.

Unfortunately, even that conscious effort to keep the peace did not diminish my sense that something was still wrong.

Thankfully I didn't have time to dwell on it because I had the urgent distraction of converting our house to suit her.

Edward suggested and I agreed to make her comfort and safety my number one priority, to aid her healing.

I willfully put my research and writing work temporarily aside only because I didn't believe anything would take as long as it did.

It took six long months of me being a project designer and manager of infrastructure just to make our home physically safe for her. At her expense we added an 'ADA compliant' ramp with hand rails, converted our atrium to a fireproof outdoor kitchen for her, and converted the common bath to a shower for wheelchair access.

She was delighted to have so much work done for her. It was all quite beautiful and efficient for her to use, and she used everything often.

However, soon after all was completed, it was obvious that it was not enough.
She commented that the new shower's water wasn't purified. She told me to bring in buckets of purified water from the reverse osmosis faucet in the kitchen.

She loathed the gritty feel of the towels I washed with baking soda and asked if I could wash them with her plant water instead.

She refused any professional manicures or pedicures because she thought I should learn to do it properly without loss of her blood.
She complained of sores on her arms and crotch but refused to use the medication the doctors prescribed.

Instead she wanted me to gather plants for her.

I was so exasperated at her density I finally said to her, "The infrastructure I have set up for you, Mother, is meant to make you less dependent on me or on anyone. That's why you don't need anyone doing all this stuff for you."
Her response was quick and aloof,
"What is so wrong about giving someone a job?"
"So you *want* someone to have the job of serving you?" I asked incredulously.
"That's part of the economy too. You should know that." She replied flippantly as she turned away to tend to her plants.
She was right of course. The economy was filled with serving jobs. There was a whole segment of employment that included serving others and I knew there was nothing wrong with that.
Then I wondered why she didn't just go hire someone else to serve her, if that's all she wanted.

It occurred to me that, unfortunately, simple servitude was not enough for a queen who also expected reverence.

That's when I realized that all my infrastructure efforts were actually attempts to change the habits of an 84 year old Queen Mother, who was more accustomed to being surrounded by loyal subjects than being self sufficient.

I laughed at my own naïveté.

It was equally futile for her to expect me to give her all that she wanted when she wanted it, though I did my best. It was part of my religion to honor my parents.

However I did not honor the containers of greenish water that she had cluttering in the new bathroom. The water molded quickly when left unrefrigerated. That on her skin would lead to nasty consequences.

I was forced to put restrictions on how much bean or leaf or whatever plant water concoctions would be permitted in the bathroom. I told her I would dump out anything moldy or in excess of the limit.

For safety reasons, I also forbade the use of glass or ceramic as food storage.

She agreed verbally, but immediately sought loopholes in the rule. She tried to wash her clothes in the bean water, which required a large bucket which she said wasn't a food storage container and should be exempt.

When I said 'okay', the bathroom suddenly got cluttered with so many large, bucket-like, vessels filled with dirty water that I said, "Enough. I will wash your laundry twice a week."

She happily agreed, but then 'helped' by washing her clothes after I already had. Then she hung them in hidden places, like under her bed and in the closet behind other clothes.

The smell of moldy bean water got so rank it became easy to find them.

To get them before they dried, I had to include looking for damp underwear in my morning routine.

The number of tasks that she could create for me to do for her seemed infinite, and even deliberate.

Therefore, I used my empathy to anticipate what she wanted. Then I got it to her before she knew what I was doing. She might be the Queen Mother, but I was the queen of labor saving, and was proud to say so.

Unfortunately, early in Mom's visit when I was still naive about her ways, I had let her buy a set of three, heavy, ceramic, bean pots.

They had since gotten onto the 'prohibited containers' list, but she promised she would only use them for storing junk. I let her keep them, but still checked them occasionally as part of my routine.

"Where is the third ceramic?' I asked Mom one day as she sat at her desk in the kitchen.

"I don't know." she said sincerely. "You did such a nice job planting that avocado out there yesterday. It looks so happy and healthy."

The compliment made me suspicious. I knew she believed it was part of my job to plant stuff for her and she had not been pleased with my planting skills.

"You agreed to keep the ceramic set in the atrium." I retorted firmly. "There are only two out there now."

"Well maybe you missed it." She said with indifference.

As I huffed down the hall to check her bathroom I called, "You know the rule about not using glass or ceramic for food storage!"

I checked the bathroom drawers and closet. I was irritated to find that she had been *hiding* the plastic containers filled with greenish water to get around my rule. Instead of getting distracted with that battle, I just emptied them and tossed the containers.

I could hear her feeble voice ask, "Now why do you need that rule again?"

"Prevention!" I yelled as I continued to search for the elusive third ceramic.

I moved back to the kitchen and stated, "You are so prone too getting pieces of glass or ceramic in your feet. I don't know if it's because you are really clumsy and drop them often, or if you are just really terrible at cleaning up. In either case, nasty foot sores can be prevented by using only plastic containers."

I thought I was being reasonable, but I think I offended her because she started grumbling.

"Big corporations make all that plastic." she taunted.

I ignored the bait meant to distract me by luring me into a pointless fight about plastic. Instead I admitted defeat and said, "Well I hope it doesn't contain anything that attracts ants because that will be a tough infestation to get rid of."

I had never before mentioned that bugs might like her bean water.

Suddenly she replied angrily, "Aw it only has water in it!"

I shot her a disapproving glance that indicated I now knew she had been lying all along.

"Where is it?" I demanded firmly.

"It's on my other desk" she said defensively as she followed me down the hall to her room. "And it's been there for three days and you never saw it even once!"

I found the third ceramic hidden behind her computer along with a large plastic container of more greenish water. Both reeked when I opened them.

I chastised her with extreme annoyance. "Do you know how this carpet is going to stink when you spill this stuff on it?"

"It's the only thing that will help my itching!" She yelled defensively as I returned all to the kitchen.

I sighed at the mention of the itching. I had been avoiding that subject until after Edward left for his trip. I didn't want to get him involved in our little battles. Now that he was away, I knew it was time.

She had been dropping hints about the itching for months, so I knew that it was creeping back.

I wondered if that 'itch' was what was brewing between us.

So I walked back to her room.

She looked so tired and helpless I decided to let her talk about her itch theories.

I was actually relieved that we were finally going to get this issue out of the way once and for all.

I sat down on a chair in her room and asked, "What's the problem? What is bothering you?"

She launched into her usual condemnation of baking soda, and how I was so cruel to wash her bedding in the stuff. She said the sheets were so useless they should be thrown out. She claimed her sores were so bad she couldn't even touch her skin. Finally, after much drama, I was sufficiently concerned that I asked to check her back.

She readily agreed, confident that it would be full of sores.

It was not. In fact her skin looked better than it ever had.

I said, "Your skin is fine, Mother. And I already told you I stopped using baking soda a long time ago. Maybe you should consider not using plant water to wash in."

She was genuinely dumbfounded and asked. "Why should I stop using the only thing that really helps?"

Her answer was stupid but I replied "Because obviously it is *not* helping and it might be aggravating."

To that she lamented dramatically. "The itching is so bad I feel like I'm going to die!"

She ranted on as she insisted even more that she knew baking soda was everywhere because she could feel it.

I could see that letting her rant was a mistake.

In fact the load of crap she was spewing was only making her more obsessed and making me more irritated.

When I had heard too much about the deadly consequences of itching, I finally stated, "You can't die from itching."

She responded with confidence like she knew she was right, "Oh really? You'll see how bad this itching gets!"

I sighed as I rolled my eyes. That prompted her to say emphatically, "Okay then I'll just drop dead!"

It was such a ridiculous statement I wanted to laugh. I said, "You are too healthy to drop dead."

"Oh that's what you think!" she replied knowingly. "You'll see! You'll see me drop dead from sheer will!"

I felt I should say something to show concern even though I thought she was being childish and preposterous. "Do you want me to take you to a hospital?" I asked sincerely.

"For what reason?" She replied incredulously.

"Well if your itching is so bad you think you're going to die," I said casually. "Then you should go see a doctor. I'd rather you not die here"

This infuriated her, "You think they can help me?! They don't know anything! And I'll die where I want to even if it's in this purgatory you have me trapped in!"

I sighed again and tried not to feel hurt. I said, "Maybe you could try a sleep aid again to…"

She didn't let me finish as she barked rudely, "I sleep fine!"

I was so tired of her tone and belligerent attitude I countered her statement with, "No, it's obvious that you have not been."

She grew angrier, "How do you know how I've been sleeping?!"

I replied "I'm very observant and you know I take notes on everything. I know you've been sleeping on your chair, and napping throughout the day. You have dark circles under your eyes."

"So what of it?" she snapped. "So I lose a little sleep. That can't cause what I'm suffering from!"

I patiently replied, "Sleep deprivation can make you feel anxious which can make you itch more."

She knew I was right because then she proceeded to mock everything I said.

She made childish faces as she meanly imitated me, "Oh you know everything! You are never, never, wrong! But I'm the ignorant, stupid, low one!"

It was incredibly tedious and offensive to watch her mock me.

She was in a frenzy and despite my bruised emotions I tried to calm her down.

I said very calmly, "No you aren't stupid Mother. In fact you are smart enough to understand that part of your itching is due to anxiety.

Maybe there is something you are really anxious about."

Her anger was swift. "Don't give me that bullshit!" she screamed. "I know what I feel! This is not in my head! You don't know anything about sin! You think *you* can show *me* what *I* already know! Well you can't! Now get out of here you stupid ass!!"

Her confounding rudeness was hard to take and I should have just walked out for my own sanity.

Yet something kept me there. Her strange words reminded me of that day in our bathroom, before she fell, when I got into her head and could see why she scratched. I remembered that I never did find the source of those 'critters' that were eating her skin.

Something in me was obsessing about that, probably because I really wanted to help her.

As I watched her fidget neurotically, perched on the little chair of purity, I could feel her crazy in my mind again and wondered if I should revisit her perspective. It was a morbid thought. I was not sure I was strong enough.

Finally I had to admit that I was in mentally unstable territory and it was best to retreat to some place that was mentally safer for me.

So I switched to thinking about where she had been.

I imagined her commune days, India, and even time with the yoga people. Those times and places were all gloriously free and enlightening but always fleeting. There was no place she could go back to. Then I saw how the place I offered, with all my rules, was terribly confining to her ephemeral spirit and it was maddening. I could feel the suffocation she must be feeling. I felt her suffering and started to cry.

I wondered if feeling her pain, from wherever she was deriving it, was also causing me to feel that weird hurt that would not go away. I felt more than ever that I should retreat from her, as everyone else had.

All these thoughts raced through my mind as I watched her try to get comfortable, so she could sleep sitting up, and without letting her feet touch the carpet.

She looked so miserable I wanted to set her free, if I could.

I finally said, "If you are so unhappy here, you know you are free to go somewhere else."

She said very woefully, as she turned to look at me. "I'm comfortable here. It's peaceful."

This statement was aggravating because she was obviously in misery. The contradiction begged so many questions. 'Did she mean she was comfortable being miserable, and in my house?' Or 'Did my house make her feel miserable and she was comfortable with that?' or 'Did I make her feel miserable?' 'And did she think that peace was the same as deep depression?'

It was hard to see anything nice in her statement.

The hurt flared up and I began to itch, so I finally gave up and walked out. It was difficult to silence all the contradictions my mother was channeling.

I was also keenly aware that my mother was making me feel increasingly schizophrenic.

One day I was washing the dishes as she sat at the kitchen window. She spontaneously stated, "Your idea for using the ceramics to hold dried herbs was excellent."
I turned to see what she was doing that would provoke her to say such a thing.
She was reading a book.
She looked happy and I freaked out. My natural reaction was to view this as a genuine compliment but instinctively knew it dangerous of me to think that.

After eight months of living with her I came to view her spontaneous kindness as a prelude to an attack.

She had a keen sense for weakness and tended to route it out at the worst times, like when I was exhausted and distracted.

That's when she would smile innocently as she was delivering a stealth mental punch.

Being honest about my feelings led to me getting sucked into an unwinnable fight with her.

I also learned, the hard way, that when she just wanted us to be 'friends', she really meant for me to be a 'volunteer slave'.

My brain froze up at all the possible traps to responding to her complement.

As she waited for me to respond with a polite 'thank you', I backed away like I was a stupid child caught in some lie.

She smiled while I ran out of the room and fled to my corner of deeply neurotic self doubt.

I knew this could not go on.

My writing work was becoming so shoddy, and I had no reasonable explanation for it.

It sounded ridiculous to say 'Mother's happiness is interfering with my research.'

It seemed that only I knew the effect she had on me. I was embarrassed that I could not stop it.

I should have just arranged to have her go somewhere else a long time ago. Everyone would understand.

I didn't want to, but I just had to call Edward. I needed his support and opinion.

"What do you think about my finding her another place to live?" I asked over the din of static. "Yes!" He yelled back. "If she's pushing you over the edge, then push back!"

"I don't want to hurt her, Ward!" I replied with concern.

"I don't want you to get hurt again!" I heard him say just before the reception got bad.

"Are you okay?" I asked. "Can you still hear me?"

After a long bout of bad reception, he said, "I can hear you but there's a lot of interference!" There were more muffled sounds before his voice came through again, "Call the boys if you need help!"

I had already thought about that and said, "They both have finals, I don't want to bother them… or see them get crushed."

My voice trailed away as I realized the danger of any of them trying to argue with Mother. She could easily provoke them to violence.

I shuddered at the though of that outcome. The phone went dead and I wondered if he heard me. It was quiet for so long I was about to end it.

Then suddenly his voice was clear. "I love you. Don't let her defeat you."

I replied sincerely, "I love you too, Ward."

The phone was silent in my hands and I was alone again.

He gave me courage, which I needed because there was more trouble ahead, no matter what I chose to do.

Chapter 13
The Epsom Salt Catapult To War

I was getting more mentally unstable as each day passed with her so close to me.

The tension in me was getting so out of control I started behaving erratically in public. It was especially bad when I went to look for places for Mom to stay and had to explain her needs. I could tell they thought I was a freak.

My work continued to deteriorate and I thought maybe I resented her for that. Maybe that was why I was feeling so damn injured.

So if I just buckled down and got my work done, then the pain would go away.

My new resolve to focus on my work led me to spend more time away from home, away from her. I did research at the library and was amazed at how productive and *normal* I was again.

However, one day when I returned home after being gone all afternoon, I could see that she had been brooding, worse than ever.

Minutes after I got in the door, she barked at me, "Get me the Epsom salts!"

I had grown desensitized to her bratty tone and asked without concern, like I was an impudent teenager, "Why can't you get it yourself?"

She glowered at me and hissed, "You took it!"

That was an unexpected response and I asked with sincerity, "Why would I take your Epsom salt when I'm the one who bought it for you?"

"I saw you take it!" she hissed. "You don't want me to have anything!"

I struggled not to lose control and very calmly walked down the hall to her bathroom still in sight of her and said, "Watch me, Mom!"

I bent down and reached into the bathroom and pulled out a box of Epsom salts. "It's right here where it's always been."

She could see the box but barked, "You just put it back!"

I would have taken the time to discern why she was so bent on fighting before asking anything of her. But then I saw that there was a message on the answering machine. It was the police. Someone had called 911 from this number.

Anger raged through me as I could see she was fine. I knew she was trying to provoke me to, well, to get angry. I resisted giving her satisfaction by commenting on the call, but it was really hard not to smack her for it.

Instead I thought about her reasons. I was on a collision course with her and I didn't think I cared what happened. So my voice dripped with caustic agitation when I asked,

"What the hell is bothering you?"

"You know you don't respect my experiences." She snapped. "You take my stuff!"

I thought for a second about what she must be thinking. It was a struggle at first to clear away all my own rational thoughts, but then, much too easily, my empathy for her kicked in. I could see her perspective again.

With a haughty air of authority which I knew she despised, I replied, "I already told you I would take the ceramic set if you kept using it for storing food or bean water. They were all filled with moldy liquid and you hid them in the closet!"

I knew instantly that I was right. She was still furious that I had found the third ceramic and then that I hid *all* three of them away.

I felt gleeful for my little victory until I saw she was gearing up for full battle for control of the containers. My little thrill evaporated. She knew I was in no condition to fight, and that, lately, I struggled just to talk to her.

I really wanted to get out of her head and get back to my own work instead.

I sorely regretted being petty.

Out of desperation, I decided to use a risky move and just act humble to appease her through distraction.

First I displayed a softened face and then asked in my best fake/sincere voice, "Why is it so important that you wash in bean water?"

She also softened her face instantly, but it would be naïve to think it was sincere. I knew she was responding to a perceived defeat.

She explained with elaborate reverence, "As God's creations, we are one with all life, even plants; all plants not just beans. We are all together part of the plant family."

"That's it?" I asked as I prepared to walk away, dismissing the goofy analogy, and relieved she was letting this one go.

She answered lightning fast, "And plant enzymes are excellent detergents."

That statement begged sarcasm, like it was bait I should have ignored. Instead I chided her lightly, "I get it. Our 'relatives' get sacrificed to extract their enzymes, so we can have clean dishes."

"We will all die anyway." She countered nonchalantly.

I thought that was a very odd statement but didn't care. I started to walk away but she was quicker.

"I've been picking leaves my whole life to test them and find what they are good for." She looked up at me expecting a victory confirmation.

I cringed at my choice of responses. Saying nothing was the same as agreeing with *all* she said. Yes, she had a wealth of plant knowledge, but her 'testing' of leaf concoctions was in no way scientific. If I simply agreed with her lame but self-aggrandizing statement, then she would launch another series of awful, useless 'plant experiments' which would bring on more containers of foul water, sores, and itching. Basically, it would make my life even more hellish.

Yet if I pointed out the stupidity of

plant water in general, she'd launch into a fight which would also make my life hell.

I instantly regretted that I falsely conceded defeat to her.
I was trapped, tired, and still hurting from some phantom wrong.
She saw my doubt and said sympathetically, "I understand that you don't know what you're doing when you dump out my plant water. You don't know any better. How could you?"

I desperately wanted to let it go and walk away, but I was losing control, worse than I ever had in my whole life. I foolishly retaliated.
"I just don't think you have proof that what you are doing is helping you." I said, coolly matching her tone. "I think it is hurting more than helping."
At those words the battle escalated instantly. She transformed from gentle to crazy with ease.

She roared "It doesn't help when you dump baking soda into my clothes to make me itch! "

"For the millionth time, I don't use baking soda anymore!" I yelled with exasperation.

"I can feel it!" she howled. "It makes my skin inflamed with itching!"

"It's not possible because there is no baking soda in your clothes!" I hissed.

"That's because I try to wash it out but you take my clothes, my underwear, after I've washed them!" she snapped harshly.

"I have to wash them because you'll get that damn crotch itch again from the bean water!" I barked with fierce anger.

She seethed with disdain and hissed "You get paid to do what I tell you! And I told you I don't need some stranger looking at my crotch. That's your job!"

That blow to my fragile emotions was swift and debilitating. I mentally slipped into my childhood place of servitude. However I still managed to inflict a feeble, retaliatory blow by saying, "You could at least try to talk more respectfully to me."

"**I** have to respect ***YOU***?!" she howled like that was the craziest thing she ever heard. "Don't you know girl, that I gave you life! I'm your *mother*! So *you* should be the one who respects *me*! God says so!"

I feebly challenged that statement, "Even if you're mean?"

"Mean?! Was it MEAN to save you from your own stupidity?!" she raged. "You say you love God but fail to honor and respect your own Mother! You **owe** me respect!"

Her crazy mental abuse was brutal and confusing. To escape it I said what I thought would appease her wrath, "I do respect you."

"You treat me like a child!" She barked back.

The word 'child' triggered something

unexpected. A mature 'stranger' inside me then replied, "Well yes, when you act like a child I will treat you like a child. When you act maturely then we can talk...but you have to stop being so hurtful, *Mother*."

This provoked her to lash out even more. She bowed down to me in mocking reverence and shrilled,
"Oh I'm sooooo SORRY *Miss Queen of know-it-all*! I'm the idiot here, even though I'm the eldest!"

She closed her eyes and pounded her hand into her fist, like she was trying *not* to smack me. Then she exploded at me as if I was saying horrible things even though I was silent.
She screamed, "Shut up! Just shut up you lazy, heartless girl!" as she threw napkins, bananas, and even her slippers around in a threatening manner.
It was bizarre and gaudy behavior which I automatically started to understand, but wholly against my

will. Unlike in the past, this time I tried desperately to stop my empathy.

It was a futile attempt. I readily assumed her dominant perspective. It was a crazy stormy view I had then. I guess I was her and me at the same time.

This volatile mix created a different, angrier, 'stranger' inside me, who suddenly bellowed as loudly as possible, "Well FUCK YOU BITCH! You can go straight to hell which I hope is run by pissed-off, brainless, fucking, bitch-monkeys and is made of fucking baking soda and plastic!"

For a moment we were both stunned by my rare display of profanities. I was utterly confused by what had just happened. The silence between us felt like the deadly calm in the eye of a hurricane. I wondered if I would survive it.

Then she broke down and cried. "You're still just like Christian! You are as schizophrenic as he is! You both scream at me that I'm a bad mother."

She sobbed skillfully, and her comparison of me to the loathsome Christian burned as it robbed me of strength and speech.
She continued. "I don't know why you both hate me! I'm only here to help you with your anger problems. Of course I understand it's upsetting that Edward left you because of your mental instability, but violence is not the answer! Don't you know I love you?"
I was tormented by her brutal response, but I wanted to kill her when she said 'I love you'.

I knew I was snapping when I reached for the large knife on the counter. Then I grew numb, with no feeling at all.
Fortunately one of the 'strangers' inside me forced me to grab the

'Neem' leaves to throw at her instead, along with rags and other random objects. It was not sufficient.

It seemed I was forced to smash a big orange on the floor and then to stamp on it repeatedly.

This still did not resolve the burning rage inside me.

Then I was rushed outside and into the bog, screaming, ranting, and horribly itching like a lunatic.

When I returned six hours later, wet, weary, and covered with insect bites, she informed me that the police had arrived and then left.

The implications made me so sick that I felt I had no choice. So I apologized and then surrendered to her, the victor.

It was a very bad war. I think the profanities made me lose it.

I was then so terrified of my psychotic and hateful behavior towards my mother that I conceded to make reparations.

I agreed to take her to buy dozens of plants. I agreed to help her dig up and transplant wild plants from the nearby woods, bogs, and fields. It seemed that the squirrels mocked me as I toiled.

I was her slave and she acted like we were buddies. She was happy for days, but I was not.

My work seemed like a long-distant memory that I would never see again. I scratched a lot.

She promptly gave me some of her bean water, like I was one of her kind now.

It was comforting to see her care for me. It made me love her so much that I sincerely tried to live in her world. But it was a fantasy.

The world had changed since I was little. I was no longer the devoted low-level catholic girl she needed me to be. Pretending that I was would disappoint her and make me miserable. So I sadly resolved to sever my deep loyalty to her, and retreat with no malice in my heart.

Chapter 14
The 'Do Over' Revolution

At that point, with my battered mental condition, I looked for refuge.

I found a small shelter in a writing class that was geared for the elderly who wanted to write their life story in six weeks. They only met for three hours, two days a week, but it was all I could manage and was better than nothing.

Mom thought I was finally keeping my promise of helping her write her biography, which I had actually forgotten.

She loved the idea of writing about herself and readily agreed to take the class. I relished the reprieve.

For her very first assignment she had to describe herself in one sentence. She wrote, "I am happy and content except when I'm always itching and viciously scratching."

Statements like those confounded me and made me question why I was still letting her live in my home.

The only answer that ever came to mind was that deep inside, I was practicing my religion.

Offering unconditional love to my mother was an obligation I had always freely accepted, though I wondered if there was an expiration date on that offer.

I loved her even though she seemed to be a source for that damn inexplicable sense of hurt that had settled in me like a broken rib.

Every day it got harder to breathe.

I stopped trying to understand why it was there and did my best to just live with the pain.

I also didn't worry anymore when she complained dramatically that she was dying from itching.

I dismissed it as an 'artistic' release that was inspired by the class, which constantly fed her appetite for drama.

For my own sake, I vowed to be polite but to stay emotionally detached when I drove her to and from the class.

However, one assignment proved impossible to ignore: She was instructed to write '10 things you would do over if given the chance and what you would do differently'.

On the drive home from that class, I politely asked her if there was anything she would 'do over'.
"I can't think of anything." She said perplexed, like everything she's done had been good.
I didn't want to pursue the subject, sensing it would not end well. So I said 'okay' and turned on the radio.

Seconds later she started talking so I turned off the radio as she said, "When I was mad at Nick I would give him the silent treatment and sulk instead of speaking up. I should have said what was upsetting me."

Surprisingly, I remembered vividly how she would pout when she was mad at Dad. I had no desire to dig up that past so, again I said 'okay' and turned on the radio.

Then I noticed she was crying and heard her say, "I was so mad I kicked him hard in the chest."

I turned off the radio for good and said incredulously, "You kicked Dad in the chest?"

"I kicked Luke in the chest!" she sobbed.

I sighed as I remembered that whole saga about her brother drowning. I thought her guilt was unfounded. Just to keep the peace I tried to remain neutral while offering her comfort. It was difficult.

"You were thirteen." I said softly. "You were just a kid."

She nodded gratefully and stopped crying, but her mind wandered to my childhood.

"Another 'do over' would be to not do so much canning!" she said emphatically.

I recalled the happy autumn days when our kitchen was filled with all of us processing the harvest from our prolific, one-acre garden. I was puzzled and asked, "What was wrong with canning?"

She replied with gusto, "I could have spent more time with you kids instead!"

I did not agree and said, "But those were fun times and you were with us for it."

She nodded as if that is what she meant.

Because of my vow to myself, I did not add that those were some of the few times that she was actively engaged with us.

I knew I was struggling to suppress the angst that was rising in me. I refused to let it out, not while I was driving, and hopefully never when she would hear it.

Instead I tried to focus on the canning days. I had to smile at the strange fun it was especially for me and Jack. The contraptions for separating the corn from the cob, for removing skins from tomatoes, and the elaborate sterilization of jars were all entertaining to the two of us who were delegated the task of manning them.

Unfortunately, my childhood revelry was interrupted by her next 'do over' statement. "Well, I would certainly deal with Christian better!"

The angst flared in my stomach because of that damn toxic weed of my life sprouting up again.

I had already forgiven the bastard decades ago. I had moved on, so there was no point in ever thinking about him.

Yet here she was bringing him back into my life like it was her mission to do so. I felt a tinge of itching.

The itching wanted to morph into rage and I could feel it welling up. It reminded me of what happened the last time I let my anger out.

I fought back with some logical thinking.

I guessed she really just wanted me to comment on her 'do overs', not necessarily on my wretched brother. I calmed down somewhat.

With great restraint I politely but reluctantly asked, "What would you have done differently?"

I did not expect any reasonable response and so was only half listening. That was until I heard her say, "I would just not listen to him, I would walk away."

Those last four words triggered an unstoppable flood of memories.

"That is what you would do differently?" I asked with thick tension which she did not notice.

Without a glance towards me she foolishly responded, "Well really,

I already learned to do that a long time ago, so it can't actually count as a do over."

When I asked, "What do you mean?" she was still oblivious of my hostility.

She seemed happy and replied almost proudly, "When you kids started fighting I found that I could take a walk out on the trails and when I returned it would all be over."

A primordial soup of confusion and white hot anger coursed through me as I was forced, it seemed, to recall the ancient events she spoke of so casually.

I could see my scared little self around age ten trying to protect the twins from Christian, who was 25ish at the time, still living at home, and who was *always* mad at us for some stupid reason. I took the brunt of his anger when no one older was around. I knew that 'the fights' were unfair, but I had no choice. Christian only attacked when Mother wasn't there to see it and he used terrifying choking tactics which never left serious marks. Whenever we had complained she dismissed it as exaggerated 'sibling rivalry', or she believed that one of us must have provoked it.

Anger was bubbling in my throat like emotional toxic waste until I finally blurted, "So you *knew* what he was doing to us?!"
She finally recognized my tone as not approving. She got stuck with her defense, "No! How could I know? I just told you that I walked away!"

Her answer felt like mockery mixed with humiliation and a kick in the gut, all together at the worst time.
Generally, it was the wrong answer.
She realized her mistake in boasting about her strategy to one of the clearly unfortunate 'kids' in those fights. Predictably for her in this kind of situation, a flood of tears was unleashed as she sobbed, "I tried everything, and no one would help me! I went to all kinds of meetings but I still didn't know what to do! Dad never helped!"

Since the memories of that time were now quite vivid in my mind, I knew she was practicing revisionism.

I shot back, "Christian needed a kick in the ass, Dad wanted to give it, but you stopped him!"

"When did I do that?" she feigned ignorance.

"Lots of times!" I responded. Yet I could not elaborate on all the confusion of that time.

My mind was bursting open as I recalled so much of my past as if it was for the first time.

I recalled how we went to that meeting called 'The Practice of Non-Violence'. In theory, non-violence was a good family policy, and initially Dad agreed to a non-violent household. We kids did do our absolute best to 'stay out of Christian's way' to avoid violence. Unfortunately, Christian found loopholes in the policy that made his violence and torture morally justified.

Back then Christian was a Catholic superstar while the youngest of us kids, especially the girls, were kind of 'low-end Catholics' without much of a future in the church.

We endured all kinds of abuse from him because we believed he was religiously superior to us.

As the youngest girl, I felt especially inferior to my handsome, brilliant, college graduate brother who was born on Christmas Day and, most importantly, was destined to be a priest. He could have ruled the world.

Eventually though, Dad was tired of the sanctimonious ass that Christian was becoming, and could not tolerate the stress anymore, and wanted him out. Mom insisted on trying all her ways first.

This all took too long and Dad's health suffered badly. It started with a series of heart attacks, then a by-pass heart surgery, and eventually removal of key internal organs that made his heart stop. He was just 68 when he died.

These recollections were my own, but I felt strangely numb and removed from them, like I was watching someone else's life.

My descent into the past was interrupted by her sobbing.

"Well it's not easy to look after so many children, especially with him away at work all day! I had the harder job!" she sobbed with deep sincerity.

Even though I was feeling immense rage, I found myself agreeing with her. I strongly wanted to reach out and hug her even as I strained to reconcile the schizophrenic feelings. Fortunately, my brain froze up and my arms would not move one inch towards her.

Then the truth became so clear it knocked the breath out of me.

I gasped, "You chose your life, Mother!" Then with fierce accusation, I continued angrily, "and you let me… a little *girl* get *tortured* by Christian, when he was a *man, twice my size*!"

Amazingly, she ignored the tragic reality I had just spelled out for her and stated quietly "I see you are angry with me."

Remembering the reparations I paid last time for my anger, I mustered all my strength to control my tone.

"I am not angry." I lied. "I just can't agree that your strategy for dealing with his... mental... illness was good."

"Oh well that is how you see it." She confidently replied. "That's fine. We all see things differently. I just know that I was helpless to do anything else."

Her indifference was maddening and I snapped angrily, "You were not just a bystander, Mother! You were the authority!"

At that she started sobbing again with amazing frailty. She skillfully cried out, "Oh so you *do* judge me as a bad mother! Well, I know that Christian was just trying to help you, and look how you treat him!"

I was in awe of her ability to go from superpower to feeble helplessness in just a few breaths. Her sobbing was so convincing that I *again* wanted to comfort her like she was a poor, misunderstood child. My brain was about to pop at the conflict. I hated that my loyalty to her was still so deep.

Her tears finally made me retreat from the fight and I said feebly, "I just don't think... I owe you... or should offer any comfort in this case."
"I'm not asking for any comfort." She insisted strongly with no sense of remorse.

It was plain to see that she was also not offering any comfort, as if no one needed it, as if no one was hurt, except maybe herself.
Something was terribly wrong inside me and my loyalty to her felt like poison.
Flashes of broken memories kept searing my mind and ignited a rage I could not suppress.
I was too dense and slow to see what was obvious: how her excuses and her

'strategy' for Christian altered *my whole life*.

All I could feel was burning hot and frightening wrath which made me physically ill. Her chronic lack of comfort was too raw to endure. Though I loved her deeply, I could not stand to be with her for another minute.

When we were finally home I turned to look at her and gagged at the morbid sight. Her arms were bloody from scratching. She had probably scratched for the whole time we were driving, they were so cut.

The sight of her blood provoked vicious homicidal thoughts. I wanted so badly to lash out at the monster I believed was sitting there, just within my reach.

Fortunately for her sake, the stranger inside me rushed me out of the car, without a strike or a word to her.

I fled into the woods, to my good place, just as I did when I was little to hide from Christian. I thought I was safe, but soon realized that the fear and panic pursued me like a vengeful demon. It seemed that he was right there beside me, still damning me to hell.

There was no escape from their condemnation. Spasms of pain gripped my body and, to my horror, I started itching uncontrollably.

I gasped for air and was sure I was dying. Nothing I could do would stop the terrifying asphyxiation. There was no one to help me as if this execution was what I deserved.

So I gave in and obediently submitted to my fate. I let the spasms evacuate the air that sustained me.

I believed it was part of the death process when all the toxic angst within me erupted out with the vomit that I so violently expelled.

When nothing else was left inside me, I looked around and sensed that I was probably not dead.

It was not a relief at all and the pain more raw than ever.

So I sat down next to my angst and cried.

I bawled my heart out for that stupidly dense adolescent girl who was only just now seeing that the one she loved unconditionally was the one who had the power to stop the hurt, but chose not to.

Chapter 15
Going Back for Her

I felt sick for weeks after the 'Do Over' fight with Bette. It was too hard to call her Mother.

She noticed that I had suddenly become depressed, distant, and wasn't eating.

She offered me strange leaves to stimulate my appetite. I refused.

I overheard her telling people on the phone that I was suffering from bad low blood sugar and was probably going to be diabetic soon because I wasn't eating enough and because I worked too hard.

It was depressing to hear her say, "Ever since she was little I had to call her my 'good little helper' because that was all she knew how to do!"

I retreated deeper into my mind.

She offered me humus. When I declined her offer, she ate all my apples and peanut butter, which she knew was my default food when I forget to eat.

When I feebly complained she said it was for my own good because the beans and humus she made would cure my melancholy.
Still I wouldn't eat.
Then she left some leaves for me to suck on, with a note, "Neem leaves are wondrous remedies and will make everything better."
Of course they were curry leaves.
Since she never said a word about the 'Do-Over' fight, it was obvious that she had blocked it out of her mind enough to be unaware of the revelation she had dropped on me.

Unfortunately, I was burned and blinded by the light she shed. The only thing I could see for weeks was the profoundly stupid little girl she was right to think I was.

She was also right that I had to eat, but I didn't care anymore. I had no hunger, no craving, and no sense to give myself nourishment. There seemed no reason to feed a stupid, useless girl.

I knew she was watching me, and was getting concerned. She continued to offer me her leaves. I did not say a word to her or to anyone. That made her anxious and nervous.

She tried to hide her scratching from me but I could see her arms. I could see her 'critters' everywhere.

I could also see that she was afraid of me, like I was a poisonous snake she wanted to kill.

She tried to call Edward but couldn't reach him.

I knew he was out of range. I noticed that she didn't try calling anyone else for help.

I lost a dangerous amount of weight, which made me get sicker, and I couldn't sleep.

I stopped writing anything, not even notes. My journals were blank, my mind was blank.

I felt dead and I was okay with that. I wanted no more knowledge, or empathy, or memories, or pain.

My new resolve was to sleep forever.

Then that stranger inside me suggested that I put some food in my belly to help me sleep.

So I ate something and then I slept for days.

But she ruled my dreams with unbearable madness and I wanted to wake up.

Then the stranger suggested I read my first diary, the one my sister gave me when I was five. She used it to teach me to write and to always take notes on everything.

But I didn't want to open up my journals. I had put them away because they were boring and painful. I laughed a little because that seemed to describe my whole life.

Then I, not the stranger, remembered that my five-year-old life wasn't painful. That was a fun time. It was worth visiting again.

I filed all my journals in chronological order so the first one was easy to find there, at the end of the box.

Reading it was like visiting a long-lost friend whom I loved and missed dearly.

My writing was clumsy then when I was five, but I could easily read the words.

'I love God, Mother, Dad, and cows.'

'I take the twins for a ride in the wagon. Bad trip, we crashed. Jack mad his wagon broke.'

'Mother say to that nun I am a good helper'.

I read how happy I felt to get her approval, but I could also see how addicting it was. Even then I cleaned, cooked, and watched the twins as much as I could just to be rewarded with her smiling praise and special names.

I got to know her so well I could anticipate what she wanted before she even asked. I learned to think what she was thinking. I obviously thought she was impressed with me, more than with the other girls.

I was safe and secure in that first diary. I didn't need to read every page. Most of it was silly kid stuff which just served to jog my memory.

That's why I hesitated to go any further. Living through shit is always bad enough. Yet, for me, to read my words would put me right back there in the shit of the places and times I fled from. It was too self- destructive to go back there again.

That's why I had put them away. That's why I turned off parts of my brain, and why there were gaps in my memory. I didn't want to know what was sad in the world. I wasn't strong enough to go through my whole life again.

But, amazingly, despite all she did or did not do, I still wanted to help her. I still wanted to find the source of her itching to stop it.

I wanted to find out why she was afraid of me.

My journals might reveal these answers.

So, if I went back in time, I would be suffering in order to discover the cure for her.
I could do that without a problem because I was raised to serve her.

My journals showed that sometime around age eleven I started writing really bad poems about everything.
My journals were littered with awful but revealing short verses.
I worked in our big garden willfully, but, according to the poem, I did not like it.

Oh work
So hard you are
In the dirt
We dig so far.

I was thrilled, however, to learn that I could get paid for hard gardening work. The plant nursery down the road had hired some of my other siblings.
Mother did not like the working idea for me. "I'm going to lose my good

little helper!" she lamented playfully.

Instead, Dad encouraged me to do some babysitting for a wealthy friend because it would pay a lot more for less time.

That's when I learned that empathy can endear me to people, especially kids. It worked so well with the little boy I babysat that his parents paid me double what they paid anyone else.

My twelfth-year journal revealed my lofty self-perception. *'Thanks to my x-ray brain I am the best babysitter in the whole world!"*

Eventually though, Mother was not happy that I was gone babysitting so much. I guess I still wasn't home enough to get all the work done. She did not ever say she was unhappy about it, but when I returned home from a job, she was often waiting for me brooding, suspicious, and sarcastic. It was confusing, and I boldly hated her attitude, as one of my poems stated.

Oh beloved Mother,
How can I love you
When I so want to hate you
As you hate my babysitting

I was not adept at being hateful. It always resulted in more work for me. I used my empathy instead. To find out what was bothering her, I would try to get into her head. I developed a process to do this, and, of course, it started with a goofy poem.

'Oh Mother,
Reverend Mother,
How can I see
What to be
To make you happier
Than a tumbleweed?

She enjoyed flowers and vegetables, so I cut and pruned them to please her.

Notes to Mother
Cabbage and roses
Peas and lavender
Harvest and prune
Today and forever

I didn't always like the tasks I saw she wanted done, as was evidenced by another poem.

The roses are blooming
The birds are chirping,
As I sit in doom
Weeding and gardening.
I am oh so, lowly, an un-holy pruner.

I even attended Mass with her on Wednesday mornings during the summer, to make her feel I was holy.

Mass is fun.
On hot summer
mornings.
Empty pews
Scary people
In the glass
Trying to get out

The messes we all made got her especially irritated. I tried to clean up after us as soon as possible. Then I wrote a bunch of poems about it.

*Spilled milk,
broken glass,
sofa forts and
dirty clothes.
Clean it up
before she cries.*

She never made me do these tasks; I did them freely.

However when I failed to do them, she let me know of her displeasure. She would have Christian do them and then scold me for causing Christian to do apparently low-level tasks.

The poem that went along with this revelation was pretty harsh considering I was only twelve.

*Dearest Mother
I have failed you
With no clean floor
I am a bane to your motherhood.*

Still, I knew she valued my efforts because she would also boast to everyone else about all that I did for her. I was satisfied with indirect praise from her.

My thirteenth-year journal got more intense. By then, Christian had become the enforcer. When any of us got rebellious or heretical, he was there to stop us, always with high drama.

He threatened horrible 'burning-in-hell' kind of things to me and my siblings. When that tactic didn't work, he humiliated us by pushing faces into the ground until we gagged for air.

I didn't judge Christian for this behavior. I thought it was his job to keep us on the 'road to heaven', but it was hard to take. I often wanted to get away, as countless poems indicated.

Dear brother
I am sorry
I cannot get to heaven
Leave me free.
And I will flee
To serenity
To branches lofty
In the willow tree.

When three of my teenaged siblings discovered that they liked beer, they started having parties in the meadow behind our house.

Even though I never heard that we couldn't drink alcohol, I guessed correctly that Christian would not approve, especially when they came home drunk.

One night, I watched from behind a chair, as Christian started to beat them for drinking. Of course, they howled back in drunken protest.

When Dad discovered what the fight was about he was furious at Christian.

"What the hell are you doing?!" He yelled as he tried to restrain Christian. "These kids are drunk!"

"That's what has to stop!" Christian yelled back, easily breaking free of Dad's grip.

"No!" Dad shouted as he then gave Christian a swift smack, "*YOU* have to stop, or you'll get them killed! "

Dad was strong but not accustomed to physical fights. His effort was not nearly enough to stop Christian's confusing rage against my intoxicated siblings. And my siblings were too unaware to know whom they were fighting. It was all so chaotic and frightening that I was sure Dad was going to die. I wanted to get mother but couldn't find her.

It was an ugly 3-way fight full of blood, alcohol, and vomit in our kitchen that night.

When exhaustion finally overcame them, they all stumbled off to bed.

I sobbed as I quickly cleaned up the mess, before mother could see it.

Then I wrote a poem about it.

Wretched filth
From bloody bowels
Mopped up sin
With holy towels

Shortly after that foul fight, Dad had the first heart attack. I was more terrified than ever that he would die.

That was when mother started reading about Gandhi and the non-violence movement. She went to meetings and learned how to do it.

She said we should practice unconditional love and non-violence towards everyone, including our brother. I obeyed mother completely because I thought Dad would die if I didn't. However, since I didn't know what unconditional love was, I asked her to explain it.

She said, "It's when you love someone no matter what they do, how mean they get, or how selfish they are. You forgive them, even if they don't apologize."

"Okay," I agreed like it was a solemn oath. "I promise to love and forgive always, no matter what. But what if he hits me?"

I remember how that question caused her to pause and look at me, like it was a loaded question.

Finally she read a few pages in the book and answered, "If someone causes you harm, then you *don't* fight back. You walk away."

I had thought about it for bit and then asked, "What if, when I walk away, he chases me?"

"You hide." She replied with a bit of irritation. "You run away as fast as you can and you hide."

That's what I did. I stayed as far from Christian as I could. I also never went with my teenaged siblings anywhere because I observed that Christian had started to follow them.
I tried to make them stop drinking to save Dad's life. They promised they would stop, but I found out that they lied. They still had parties and Christian still got mad about it.

So I vowed not to drink, like I thought they would all follow my lead. To Christian that vow looked virtuous, but everyone else knew it was easy because alcohol gave me really bad headaches. Still, it helped me stay out of trouble with Christian.
One poem revealed that my life then was a balance of appeasing my holy brother, saving Dad's life, pleasing Mother, and being thirteen.

Wretched me.
Lowly bane
to holiness.
Failing.
To ease your mind
is my greatest wish.

But Christian wanted undivided loyalty. He threatened damnation if we did not consent. Since I had no idea what specifically he wanted us to consent to, I used empathy to guess.

I gathered that he didn't care what my brothers did, but he wanted me and my sisters to be nuns. Even as a devout Catholic, at thirteen I was still foggy on how, exactly, to be a nun. I saw that scoffing to Christian about becoming clergy got my siblings hellish grief and warnings that their attitude would put them on the road to hell itself.

To avoid their fate, I learned to say things that *sounded* like I wanted to join a nunnery. I was guilt-ridden for my deception, as another poem showed.

Help me please
I'm dying.
I cannot ease
With lying
That a nun would be fun
To be for me
Help me please I'm dying.

I didn't let my guilt cause me to change my strategy. He believed I was sincere in my words, enough that he left me alone, for awhile anyway.

Later on, after all my sisters moved out to go to college, I was the only girl left and suddenly the only focus of Christian's attention.
When boys started to call me, Christian got enraged. That's when he really began reminding me of my vague vow to become a nun.

I did not want more fights with him. I had witnessed too many already, and Dad was getting sicker, despite my adherence to non-violence and unconditional love. That was why I could not simply tell Christian that I only 'implied' that I would be a nun. It would definitely start a war.

Yet, it was getting more difficult to evade the subject.

I didn't know how I could phrase the truth in a nice, holy way.

So I tried to talk to my very pious Catholic girl classmates whom I thought were my friends, but that did not go well.

They never gave me a chance to explain my dilemma. While we were sitting at the lunch table, before I could take a bite of my liver sausage sandwich, they informed me that everyone could see I had 'boobs'.

I instinctively glowered down at my chest with disdain.

They continued to explain that my boobs were giving the boys bad ideas.

They couldn't give me any more details and they thought I should go to confession for my problem. I said that I didn't even tell them about it yet. They replied that my boobs were my problem and then they ate lunch outside without me.

I guessed that my breasts were shameful but I was not going to tell a priest about them. Instead I tried to flatten them, which was very awkward. When breathing became difficult, I had to abandon that tactic.
I resigned myself to living with my shame as best I could.

The result was that the good girls avoided me and the bad boys hounded me cruelly and relentlessly. I was miserably stuck smack in the middle of that impossibly Catholic world.

That's when I started to confide in my mother. She always sat in the same sunny spot of our kitchen that opened to an equally sunny porch. Every day after school the twins would sit in the sun and tell her about their day. She listened happily to them and laughed often.

I wasn't sure how she would react to what I had to say. I timidly told her a little about the boys in my class, but not the boob part. That seemed unchaste.

Since she was watching me and nodding I thought she was listening. I felt relieved that someone understood me. For awhile I talked to her every day about school. She never said much, but I didn't expect much. It helped just being able to talk about it.

Then I realized that when she was nodding, she was nodding asleep, with her eyes partially open so it looked like she was awake.

Of course that was discouraging, but I kept talking anyway, kind of to myself. However, I lost motivation to talk to her when, one day, she woke up while I was talking. I was staring at the ceiling as I mused about my day and was casually stretched out on the chair with my legs spread and wearing cream colored jeans under my school uniform skirt.

Her gasp caught my attention immediately. I looked at her and saw she was very alarmed.

"What is it?" I asked with concern.

She leaned over and whispered in my ear, "I need to talk to you about something they call 'a period'. It is something that girls get when they aren't virgins anymore."

I was stunned from embarrassment and confusion. Words came out of my mouth anyway. "What are you talking about?"

She pointed at my legs and said, "You have stains on your crotch. You must be having your first period. "

Her statement revealed how little she knew of me and how little she listened to me, but I was not angry. I didn't have to look at the stains. Instead I replied very slowly and carefully, "No, Mother, it's rust from Mark's bike. I rode it home from school. I had my first period when I was eleven. And it has nothing to do with being a virgin."

That was the first time I ever saw disdain in her face. It was a shock to see, so I remembered it vividly when she replied coolly, "Don't be impudent. You should know that the start of menstruation means that you can get pregnant. You're an adult in the eyes of God now. If you're going to be a nun you better listen to Christian, and stop hanging around those boys and keep yourself covered, instead of walking around letting it all hang out like you do. "

Before the sting of her cutting and unfair words could have an impact, I heard a smug kind of grunt from just outside the screen door. I looked and quickly caught a glimpse of Christian right at the corner of the porch. He was standing hidden next to the large post but his shadow and an arm were easily visible.

He must have been standing there the whole time, maybe even every day that I talked with Mother.

The embarrassment that seeped deep into my bones made me weak and I could not reply or even speak. I did look at her though and I remember her face. It was victorious. She mistook my embarrassment for defeat.

I assumed then that she did not know Christian was there. She must not have heard him laugh at me and I did not expose him.

I did not blame her. I blamed myself for correcting my Mother so boldly and with disrespect.

I thought it was arrogant of me.

She was right. Menstruation meant I could get pregnant. Even though I was unsure how that worked I knew she was trying to warn and protect me.

As for Christian, she always said she could not know where he was all the time. It was not her fault if he spied on me.

I stopped confiding in her anyway and I started mistrusting everyone. I wrote a baleful poem that marked the beginning of my habit of imprudent silence.

He lies in the shadows
listening for my fall.
So I'll send my words
to heaven now
or to none at all.

Chapter 16
St. Mary's Haven

I remembered how the pressure from the boys became unbearable. It was all the more embarrassing because I strained to suppress my own volatile hormones at fourteen. The poem said so.

Shameful skin
Like silos of sin.
Always rising
To meet their eyes,
To be Catholic is a miracle.

Both home and school became hellish for me. Even if a nice boy dared to call me, Christian would pull the phone cord out of the wall.

When some of the boys came to visit me, he chased them off like a crazed Yeti. That's what they called him at school.

At night he would rant for hours to my mother about how I was becoming a slut just like Madeline.

215

I started eating pounds of school 'fund raising' chocolate and then suffered severe acne everywhere. I got no sleep. My hair was greasy all the time. I grew chronically paranoid, and eventually I developed nervous chest pains. I looked and felt like a freak.

The convent was looking like my only escape from hell.

I was getting so desperate for him to stop the rants I stated plainly that I was looking into 'the orders'. I said that there was an all-girls Catholic high school that was run by nuns. It had a convent on school grounds.

Thankfully, Dad agreed that it would be a good choice and began to make the arrangements.

This quieted Christian sufficiently that I got some regular sleep again. My acne cleared up, and I prayed that I would like the new school.

St. Mary's was a haven for me because there were no boys to pressure me or to make Christian suspicious.

I was happy to find that many of my classmates were pregnant, because then I was not judged so harshly for having womanly boobs.

I loved school again. I took as many classes as I could, studied hard, and got good grades. I excelled so rapidly that I was on track to graduate as a junior. I was thrilled that I might get to start college at seventeen, as Dad had done.

It was there that I took my first economics class, and also when I talked to Dad the most.

That's when I realized he was a kindred spirit. I was genuinely happy and at ease when I was with him, even though he was still quite sick. Talking about money theory got his mind off his health problems for awhile, and I was grateful to oblige him. I was also impressed at how much he knew about the economy. I suggested that maybe we could write a book about it, together. He really liked the idea and I was overjoyed.

I guess I never got around to that.

I was just fifteen, and it was a very different world I was in then, one that I never wanted to leave.

However, Mother and Christian seemed to be uneasy about the time I spent with Dad. They did not understand what we were talking about and tried to discourage it.

So I began thinking sincerely about the convent because it would make everyone so happy.

I decided I'd research it more first before saying anything to Christian. Since he was still kind of stalking me, I didn't want to upset him again if I decided not to.

I went to the Mother House to discover the world of the nunnery.

From the talk with the Reverend Mother, I learned that nuns are servants of God. I don't know why, but that idea just cracked me up. I asked if she meant that God needed domestic help to cook and clean for him. The Reverend Mother had no sense of humor. She replied with a dour face that, "God needed someone to serve the poor and the elderly. The 'Sisters of Perpetual Morning' provide for the aged when they get sick."

She gave me a tour of the old and richly decorated building that used to be a boarding school.

It became obvious that the residents were mostly priests who didn't look old or sick enough to be there. All the 'servants' were nuns, with the exception of the Reverend Mother, whose job was to manage all the low-level nuns. I noticed that she was adored by all the priests.

I laughed out loud at the chauvinistic goofiness of it all.

I was amazed that none of the women noticed the gender breakdown of their roles. It was exactly like what I had just read about for my medieval history class: The priests were the lords and the nuns were the vassals.

"Is something funny?" the Reverend Mother asked, interrupting my train of thought.

"I'm just…" I waited, with a strained smile, for the right words to come to me, "I'm just happy to see that these good priests are being given such care in their old age."

She accepted that explanation and agreed, "Yes, we are content in our mission to be completely devoted to the well-being of the servants of God. You could be very content here too if you so choose."

I nodded but kept my mouth shut tight. I politely excused myself to go to class.

I knew that convents were not all the same as this one was, but it made me nervous anyway.

I was especially pained to think about Christian's reaction if I decided not to join. I evaded the subject entirely until the following semester when I took an advanced biology class. That's when my head really cleared.

The class was taught by the most amazingly gorgeous man I had ever seen in my life. He was perfect in every way. Every girl in the class wanted to marry him, including me. That's when I knew I could never be a nun.

Christian guessed my change of heart. It became especially obvious when I started talking about Thomas More.

At first he thought I was talking about the 16th Century Catholic writer. Then he caught on that I had been spending time at the all-boys Catholic school, which had recently been re-named 'Thomas More'. I discovered that it was an easy walk to get to, through the wooded convent grounds. He was furious when I got a female lead role in their school play.

That's when he started calling me profane names I had never even heard before. We got into stupid fights over TV shows and movies I wanted to see.

I had grown quite strong by then because of having to fight him so much. So when he pushed me, I started pushing back. He viewed this tactic as scandalous and very disrespectful.

He grew dark and more frightening than ever before. So I tried to stay away from home as much as possible. It only made him more suspicious.

The rants began again and so did sleepless nights for everyone, even Dad. I so much wanted to confide in Dad, but his health was getting so bad I couldn't, wouldn't burden him with the awful details of what Christian was saying just to me. Dad still believed Christian was going to be a priest someday.

I was growing skeptical about that and even made a few bold comments to Christian about it which only infuriated him, of course.

I started to hate him and didn't care about hurting his feelings. Our fights grew worse.

So, to avoid fights with Christian, Mother encouraged me to stay with my sisters during that summer.

She said sweetly, "It would help Dad if there was not so much fighting here."

It did not occur to me that she should be asking Christian, who was twenty-eight, to leave, and not me, who was just fifteen.

Instead I thought she was being a cool mom by letting me stay with my sisters, in a lower flat, on a college campus, with thousands of young, cute college guys when I looked like I did. No one believed me when I told them my real age. A driver's license would have been proof, but I didn't have one because I wasn't old enough yet. I didn't even have a temporary one. They thought I was hiding my license because it would show I was not old enough to drink.

My sisters did not care what I did. They said that they weren't my babysitters and they trusted me.

So at first I went to lots of parties.

It was great fun until the guys I liked wanted me to drink with them. I was not opposed to alcohol. I suffered wine every Sunday at Mass for years. It was that alcohol instantly gave me such horrible headaches, I couldn't tolerate the pain. They didn't believe that excuse either. Instead I was labeled 'Catholic prudish' and just forgotten. Those two weeks of rejection and loneliness were tortuous.

I grew depressed enough to consider talking to Mother about it. Then I realized that she had not once called me in the six weeks I was gone! I had talked to Dad only because when I called, he answered the phone. I guessed that she didn't call me because he let her know I was okay. I was very reluctant to talk to him about boys, though in retrospect I should have.

So I talked to Madeline instead.

She set me straight. "Are you crazy?!" she said frantically. "You can't 'date' college guys! You are a minor!"

"What does that mean?" I asked naively.

She was exasperated, "It means that they'll get arrested, and you could get pregnant before you reach sixteen!"

"Oh." I said, still not fully understanding how dating could get me pregnant. I didn't dare ask because she was already so mad at my questions and I felt very stupid.

After some long walks along the lake I decided that I wouldn't 'date' because I didn't want these guys to get arrested just for being with me.

But the main reason for not 'dating' was my fear of getting pregnant, and being like so many of my classmates who did not go on to college because of it.

To occupy my time I got a job in a bakery that was just down the block from my sisters' flat.

That was the first time I learned that using empathy could be dangerous.

I wanted to do a good job as a baker. So, as usual, I asked a lot of questions to discern what the boss wanted so I could give it to him.

It was just like I did at home and with babysitting.

But this was not the same. He completely misinterpreted my job interest. He thought my playful, probing questions were evidence of my personal interest in him.

He accepted what he thought were romantic advances and awkwardly tried to reciprocate.

Neither of us was very bright.

I was so dense I did not know what he was doing when, one day after work, he gave me a long sweaty hug. It was quite gross.

I thought he was gripping me so hard because he was having a heart attack, and maybe even passed out.

So I quickly pushed him away hard. His eyes were glassy and staring like in fear. So I lowered his 200 pound body to the floor with ease, and started to do something like CPR. I felt so sorry that he might be dying so I sobbed a bit.

The man was, of course, not dying. He was shocked, and then afraid of how freakishly strong I was.

I lost the job. I never told Mother what happened, but I should have.

When I came home for school I found

my absence had made Christian monstrous. He was convinced I had been having sex with college guys. I wanted to scream at him that I didn't even know what sex was, but the thought of that fight was ghastly.

I did my best to ignore him and the topic of sex.

My only real option was to again stay away to avoid fights with Christian.

I got a job at a pizza place. Almost the same thing happened as the last time I used my empathy to learn what to do on a job.

Apparently I sent sexual overtures to the manager, who was married to the assistant manager, who was offended that I was behaving like a slut towards her husband.

She insisted that I be let go. It was a tedious job anyway.

So in order to be frequently away from home, I tried out for another play at Thomas More.

I got the part. Edward was the male lead opposite me. He was smart, handsome, and Catholic too. We spent loads of time talking and exploring the wooded convent grounds overlooking the lake.

He was not deterred when I told him about my brother, but he was worried for me. He gave me strategies for defeating an opponent. I fell in love, life was good, and I thought I was truly on the road to heaven.

Chapter 17
A Good Catholic Mother

As I read the journal that approached my seventeenth year I grew tense and reluctant.

My memory of it was murky, but I knew my journal would be starkly clear.

I braced myself for more pain.

I read about how Christian hated that I was still with Edward after six months. He still wanted me to be a nun, and had little to do but obsess about it.

I did my best to show him (but not tell him) that I could still be a good Catholic without joining a convent. I went to church regularly and attended almost all of the Catholic protest rallies.

Strangely, it was mostly Mother who was not satisfied. She grew more cantankerous towards me, despite my efforts to please her.

She seemed especially disdainful of my talk of college. Whenever I brought it up, she just nodded without any comment. For her, that was a sign of disdain.

In contrast, she loved it when I talked about Edward's youthful ideas for building a hovercraft.

She asked lots of questions about his plans to use it to fly to Canada so he could live in the tundra, but also fly back to visit family whenever he wanted. He was seventeen.

She also asked about our ideas for a new church. It was a new idea to us, so I didn't have much to say about it. Plus, I knew it would get Christian really mad. It annoyed me that she would bring that up when he could be listening. He had enough reasons already to despise Edward.

When I didn't have anything exciting to talk about, she seemed to want me outside. She still had endless outside tasks for me to do, like pruning the bushes, tending the garden, or collecting plants for her from the field. I guess she was trying to keep me separate from Christian to minimize conflict.

It had been a particularly cool, wet spring and early summer. I grew tired of being out in the damp all the time. Being confined indoors with Christian was unbearable.

So I spent a lot of days and some nights at Edward's house.

Then Dad had another heart attack. He was in and out of the hospital a lot. So I reversed myself, and decided I should be at home more for Dad's sake. I helped him when he needed things Mother or Christian did not provide.

I admit I was also being selfish when I chose to help Dad. I had fulfilled all my graduation requirements and, since I was still a minor, I needed him to sign the documents for my early graduation and for admission to college.

That was a long process that involved a lot of paperwork and money.

I knew I was the only one who gained from this goal. So I didn't want to pressure Dad to help me when he was recovering from major surgery. When the timing was right I would remind him of my plans. He was supportive and as helpful as he could be under the circumstances. But at that time it was not a high priority for him.

I reminded Mother too, but she was so forgetful I had to explain the policy to her every time.

I watched the mail for important documents she might throw out. That's why I stayed home more. I wanted to wrap up my high school and get to college as soon as possible. I was so close it seemed nothing could be big enough to interfere.

However, my journal indicated that the more time I spent at home the more Christian disdained me and my plans for college. He stated several times that a nun did not need to go to college, at least not until after I was committed. Then I could learn whatever I wanted about the church.

He remained willfully ignorant of my obvious choices.
Ever since I fell in love with Edward, I had resolved that I would stop implying any interest in the convent.
One poem described how tense things had gotten between me and Christian.

Bonds straining
Wills clashing
Missions failing
Truths crashing
He will not win my soul.

His attempts to force his will on me culminated in a particular outburst that occurred on a cloudy day in late September.
Dad had been out of the hospital for a few months and was doing better, but he got tired easily. So when we had returned from church, he went right into the house to take a nap. Mother had stopped to assess the robust arching rose bush that was still encroaching on the front door that late in the season.
I was just getting out of the car.

Suddenly, Christian ran out from the side of the house, like he had been waiting for me to be alone. He jumped in front of me and furiously kicked me in the stomach.

It knocked the wind out of me but I wasn't hurt. I was still freakishly strong.

I didn't protest or retaliate. I just watched as he ranted.

"That's to stop your sin! To stop the pregnancy!" He yelled as he retreated sporadically. "You should thank me! I saved you from purgatory! I saved you from embarrassment of being an unwed mother!"

I did not flinch at his offenses because, by then, my shell was thick. Nothing he said hurt me.

When he finally ran off back behind the house, I ran up to mother who I knew had seen the whole thing.

Still I challenged her, "Did you see what he just did to me Mother?"

"Well," she shrugged her shoulders, "sibling rivalry can take strange forms."

I remember that I had not accepted that answer. Instead I stood my ground, kept silent, and stared at her.

She and I both knew that what Christian had done was terribly wrong. By Catholic standards he had committed a mortal sin since Catholics do not terminate pregnancies for *any* reason.

Even Christian knew his words, actions, and especially his intent comprised a serious sin, regardless of the outcome.

He also knew that this was not the first time he had sinned against me or his other sisters.

His boldness seemed to show that he *wanted* someone to stop him.

There was no doubt that the right choice was to reprimand him, 'the Holy One', and defend me the stupid, slutty girl.

I could see, from this distance of time, that I was forcing Mother to make that loathsome choice. Furthermore, despite her claims, she did have the authority and power to stop him.

I read her response to my silent stare without needing to.

I would never really forget her arrogant look of indifference and her words to match.

She asked dismissively, "Well, *are* you having sex?"

My response revealed my ignorance of the real situation.

"I'm a good Catholic mother." I fumbled and she laughed at my clumsy choice of words and misplaced emphasis.

"You're a good Catholic mother already?!" she mocked. "Is that your way of saying that you *are* pregnant, like your classmates?"

"No!" I defended myself, "I meant to put a comma after… Catholic."

My voice trailed off because I could see she was growing impatient with me and was not listening.

She stated, "Just answer the question. Are you having premarital sex like all your sisters have done?"

That revelation actually surprised me and I wondered if it was true. But I didn't have time to ask because I could see she was waiting for my answer.

"No!" I replied with deep embarrassment, "I am not having sex with Edward."

She still waited with judgmental eyes. I gave her the response she wanted. "I'm not having sex with Edward or *with anyone*."

She peered at me for awhile before she said arrogantly, "Well, if there is no pregnancy then no mortal sin was committed."

With that final judgment of the issue, she abruptly turned away from me, and right into a thick of long, thorny rose stems.

She was startled at being so close to the rose bush. The bramble scratched her arms, and she winced at the blood that was staining her blouse.

I was surprised that the thorns were that sharp. In all the times I had pruned that rose bush I had never gotten scratched enough to break the skin.

In her attempt to disentangle herself, she managed to get both of her arms scratched so badly they were bleeding everywhere. She scolded me for not pruning it enough. Forgetting her crushing statement to me, I quickly helped her out of the brambles. "I'm sorry." I said "They just looked so beautiful I thought it could stay like this for awhile."

I helped her into the house and then ran to get alcohol and a bandage for the wounds. She rested silently until I was finished.

At that time I believed that her decree of Christian's innocence was justified because I was not actually pregnant.

Yet, in retrospect, I could see that I was lying to myself. I knew she was in error because the intent of his actions was the sin. The fact that there was no conception did not absolve him of it.

Yet I chose not to challenge it. I preferred to stay in her good graces, which I decided would be more beneficial to me. We both knew that the matter was not resolved that day. And we both let it fester for the subsequent decades.

The next twenty pages of my journals were filled with rambling lamentations about why she had become so hostile to me, and how I tried to get her love back with empathy.

I condemned myself for never being around to cook or clean anymore like she wanted. It was ridiculously adolescent of both of us, especially since I was almost an adult and college bound.

Buried in all that crap I found some poems that showed how the rose bush incident was still bothersome.

Please understand
I am a woman
Not your handyman.
I need to live my life
Instead of pruning
That dumb rose bush.

Eventually the rose bush had been pruned to death, but not by me.
Since no one confessed, it was a mystery for awhile, until I figured it out who did it.
A poem showed that I knew who was responsible for its demise but not why it had to die.

Dear holy brother
Your sin
Is exposed.
The rose bush is dead.
Mother confessed
 you did it.
She does not lie,
About plants.

I guess she told him to just get rid of the wicked rose bush that reminded her of things she wanted to ignore.
But instead of digging it up completely like she wanted, he only pruned it severely, causing it to suffer a slow, embarrassing death.

I humbly questioned her about it.

Oh Mother,
Dear Mother
So sorry I am
For cuts so deep
That made you weep
From thorns so damned

Oh Mother
Dear Mother
So grateful I am
my womb is spared.
His guilt you cleared
So why reprimand
a rose bush for our sins?

There were also entries about Christian getting much worse, but not towards me, towards Mother.
I think he was chastising her for not punishing him.

He hounds you for penance
He begs his conviction
But for the sins of a son
you grant only sanction.

Of course, the day of the rose bush incident wasn't the first time he sinned, or the first time she defended his offensive actions.

It was, however, the first time she had such an innocent witness to her abuse of power, and one who took notes on everything. I think it was the beginning of her shunning of me.

Chapter 18
Why She Left Home

When I turned seventeen, Christian was still at home and I was not a nun.

He persisted in believing there was still hope for me. He claimed that with special permission from our parents I could sign up early, before I was an adult.

I knew I still could not reveal my true feelings about that matter so I evasively turned the question back to him.

"Why aren't *you* in the seminary already?" I boldly asked.

That angered him and he swung his fist at me which I only narrowly dodged. I really wasn't being mean. I genuinely wondered what he was waiting for. Dad had told me long ago that Christian had been accepted at a good seminary and everything was set for him.

"Who will save your soul if I go?" was typical of the answers he gave to me and anyone else who bothered to ask.

It was not clear how the two goals were mutually exclusive. In fact his efforts to 'save us' were obviously making him more violent and extreme and so, *less* eligible for the priesthood.
He was not an ignoramus. He must have known what he was doing, but didn't share his real reasons with us.

However I did know that, in his mind, I needed 'saving' the most.
The fact that I was with the same boy after more than a year was enough evidence to prove I was going to hell.
It made him fly into constant rages.
One memorable rage session was worthy of describing in my journal because it marked a change in my strategy for dealing with him.

A common tactic of his was to follow me into places that had just one escape which he could block. In this incident, he followed me to the basement laundry room. Then, when he was sure I was alone and trapped, he proceeded to scream at me, "You're worse than your sisters! You're all sexed-up sluts but *you* couldn't even wait until you left home!"

A few years of this kind of crap had forced me to shut off my feelings and ignore his insults.

However, coaching from Edward encouraged a different response. "If you lay one finger on me," I looked Christian straight in the eye, "I will call the police."

He backed down and departed quickly. I was relieved because I did not want to call the police.

I thought it would make Dad more stressed.

Unfortunately, a few days after that incident, Dad had been admitted into the hospital again because of some serious complications. There was nothing we could do but let the doctors do their job to make him better. We all went home.

A few days later Christian confronted me in our kitchen. This was unusual because I was neither trapped nor alone; Mother was present.

I guess he wanted her to hear this case. He accused me, within earshot of Mother, of trying to provoke him to anger with the threat of calling the police on him. He said I was being impudent and irreverent to a lay clergy. He demanded an apology.

It was news to me that he was a secular member of the clergy, but it did not alter my resolve to stand up to him. "It's a sin to hurt your fellow man." I stated.
"You aren't a man," he mocked me.

I walked away from his stupid game and he chased me. This was a familiar and tedious battle that I was not going to continue. As I dodged his blocks to my path I ran to stand behind Mother, who was sitting in her sunny spot reading a book.
"Mother," I pleaded seriously, "Please would you make him stop bothering me."

She didn't even look up but said, "You kids can work out your own problems."

"He's not a kid, Mother!" I replied as I pushed a chair into his way that caused him to lose his balance and her to drop her book. He howled in protest at me while she scolded me for disturbing her. "Take your fight somewhere else!" she growled.

He added as he staggered to his feet, "Yeah, go to the convent where you belong!"

Mother snickered and I grew fiercely angry.

"No!" I yelled in frustration as I ran out into the hallway.

"Girl," He bellowed like he was some holy-roller preacher, "you'd better do what's right or I'll give you such a one!"

His habit of pestering and threatening me during his rants increasingly provoked me to match his rage. He chased me into the hall, so I retaliated by slamming a door in his face.

Of course that only escalated the war, but my anger was blinding me to logic. My rage also made me careless about the words that came out of my mouth. It never seemed that anyone listened anyway.

"Stop chasing me!" I screamed. "Just leave me alone!"

"Not until you agree to be a nun!" He countered as if it was a reasonable negotiation.

He tried to corner me but I slipped away through the door to the winding stairs.

"I don't want to be a nun! I never wanted to be a nun and I'm never going to be a nun!" I screamed as I fled to my room upstairs where he usually never followed.

So when I got to the top I rested to catch my breath.

Then to my horror, I saw him bounding up toward me with amazing speed and fury. That's when I realized that he *did* listen to me once in awhile and I had just revealed my true feelings to him about the convent.

More damning was that it looked like I had been lying to him for years.

I instantly regretted my horribly timed words. I ran to the bathroom and locked myself in.

He pounded fiercely on wooden door with rusty hinges, screaming "You lying slut! You are so sexed-up you are going to suffer such torment for it!"

I felt sick to my stomach and desperately wished I could undo the last ten minutes.

It was the worst I had ever seen him in my life. I tried to threaten him again, "If you touch me I will call the police!"

"Call the police!" he screamed back. "Go ahead! I'll tell them how much you lie! I'll tell them how you slammed me with a hammer and cut me up with a knife! I'm all bloody because of you! That's what I'll tell the police!"

This was a new and alarming strategy for him to use. I was roughly his height and size. The police might believe him. I tried to think if anyone else was home. The twins were at work and Jack was never around anymore. Mother was the only witness, and she was downstairs. I wondered whom she would support.

He was pounding harder on the door as he ranted incoherently.

"If you aren't a nun then you are nothing in the eyes of God!" I heard him say, as if taunting me.

When I screamed for Mother he screamed louder. "You whore yourself out to everyone else! Don't you know anything?! Don't you know what you are giving up?!"

"Go away!" I screamed.

"I'm your elder!" he thundered. "You listen to me! You do as I say! It's for your own good!"

Years of accepting his false authority over me made me even angrier and so repulsed that I lost control.

"Bullshit!" I stupidly countered. "You can go straight to hell, you fucking bastard!"

I hated my words which just fueled his rage.

He roared more fiercely, "That kind of language proves you are a sexed-up whore!" He put his fist almost through the door as he screamed, "and sex like that should stay within the family!"

Those words stopped me cold.

The bulge in the door and the loose hinges were wrenching reminders of the real danger I was in. Strong as I had become, I knew I was no match for his enraged strength. Begging was my best chance.

"Please, Christian," I sobbed, "I'll be good!"

"You're lying!" He roared and slammed his body against the door.

"No, I'm not," I whimpered. "I… was lying before."

"Prove it!" he bellowed and pounded on the wall causing pieces of plaster to rain down on me.

"I don't know how!" I frantically sobbed. "How can I prove anything?"

He raged on about all the evils of sex and why it should only be within the family. "Then sex would be pure!" He bellowed again with new force and the wall shuddered.

I braced for the imminent collapse of the feebly hung door that was all that separated me from his madness.

I kept silent as he pounded.

But to myself I was frantically repeating 'Don't get raped.'

Over and over I mouthed the words like I was reading a confusing part of an instruction manual.

Then I noticed the pounding had stopped, the dust was still in the air.

I listened for breathing outside the door. He could have been waiting for me to come out or maybe he had fallen asleep from exhaustion.

I strained to catch any sound at all but I could hear nothing. I thought maybe my silence convinced him that I had escaped out the bathroom window.

Even if this was true, I knew from the

past episodes, that he *always* got a second wind. This fight could go on far into the night and could end more tragically than anything that preceded it, especially since he felt it was his religious duty to enforce his plans for me.

I still hesitated and listened for sounds of his presence, while I thought of what to do next.

Knowing that no help would be available to me, I decided I could not wait for help to arrive.
That was when it sunk in that I had to leave, not just for the day, but for always.
I cried for a few minutes, knowing what I was probably leaving behind.
But there was no time to grieve. He could return to put an end to *any* dreams I had for myself.

Then I brushed myself off, very quietly opened the door, and peered out into the hall through to the bedrooms.

He was not in sight.

I gathered a few of my things, a little money, and I climbed out a bedroom window. I scrambled across the roof, slipped down the trellis, and ran away without ever looking back.

I never lived at home again.

Chapter 19
Shutting Out the Light

It was cathartic to read about why I made the exodus from home. I had forgotten.

I didn't go to stay with Edward because we weren't married.

Instead, I asked Mary, my oldest sister, if I could stay with her and her husband for awhile. She agreed, but it was hard.

For the first few weeks I was in denial about what had happened.

My journal entries were sickly sweet accounts of peace, love, and God.

It wasn't until three weeks later that there was mention of any communication with Mother.

I called her to see how Dad was.

She said he was in the hospital again and couldn't be bothered with news about sibling rivalry.

"I understand." I humbly conceded. "But I can visit him, right?"

"Of course," she said kindly. "He would like visits from all his children."
I was quiet for a moment, and then tried to broach the sensitive subject. "Did you know that I'm staying with Mary for awhile?"
"Yes," she said enthusiastically. "Mary called and told me all about it a few weeks ago."
"Are you… um…" I fumbled over my words "are you… did you tell… um does…"
She stopped me and said, "It sounds like everything turned out alright, except that I lost my good little helper."

Reading that conversation in my journal helped me understand what a real mess I had been in.
By my own choice, I was homeless at seventeen, and my mother was not going to ask me back.
In her eyes, and in the eyes of God,
I was an adult, and that is exactly how she treated me. School was my problem.

Tragically, my ingrained loyalty to her trumped this cold harsh reality, and also caused me to practice more imprudent silence.

I could have told everyone the truth; that my brother was trying to rape me because I would not be a nun and my mother did not try to stop him.

I had planned to go to the Reverend Mother with my dilemma. I remember practicing how I would explain to her what happened. I tried so many versions and none of them came out right. It was like trying to talk to my grade school classmates. I could imagine no scenario that would be helpful to me. I thought that all my choices for defense would change nothing, yet would include deep humiliation for me and great hurt for many others, especially for Dad.

The next poem expressed my final decision to blindly protect her and shut out the past.

Dear Mother
He needs you more

Than I ever could.
His rants and rage
Are cries of pain.
Save his life for me
And I will fade away for you.

'I'm so happy that she is not mad at me for leaving. I love her so much.'

Yet I was not happy for myself. It was a heart-wrenching time as doors slammed shut everywhere I turned. School, which I also loved so much and which had been so close, was slipping away.

I suddenly had nothing left, but I could not complain because I apparently chose freely the path I was on.

And it was cold. The only warmth in my life was with Edward, whom I loved dearly as well.

I clung to him like he was the only person left in a bitterly frozen world.

I sighed at my plight, which was so much easier to see from a safe distance.

It helped me see that Mother was right; I had something inside me that made me determined to make the best out of any crappy situation.

My life after that was a process of denial, as well as a search for a new path. Several journal entries indicated many precarious adventures. Some were very hard to revisit.

-*'Dad was very mad at me because Edward and I have left school so we can start our own church.'*

-*'He said "What about our book? When will we get started on that? I'm not going to be around forever, you know." Dad doesn't understand me anymore.'*

-*'Mary is opposed to us starting a church and she told me to find somewhere else to live.'*

-*'Good news! God showed me a place to live! Two nice, foreign-speaking men agreed to pay me a lot of money to be their live-in maid! It's okay. They said they were Catholic, so I trust them.'*

-*'Sadly, Edward's mother said I should live in their guest bedroom instead. I didn't want to live in his family's house until we were married. Plus, I don't have a job now.'*

-'Good news! I got a job at the Buddy Nut Squirrel Shop!

'Sadly, I lost the BS nut shop job because I kept getting the name mixed up when I answered the phone. I strongly dislike squirrels.'

-'Our church is going well. We have 2 new members!

-Edward asked me to marry him and I said yes.

-'Edward turned 18 and now we are married!

Unfortunately, the two new members we used as the witnesses got mad. They thought we were meeting to plan a revolution, like what Martin Luther did in the 1500s but with Hover Vehicles featured in Popular Science magazine. I guess Edward implied this would happen if they joined.'

-'I have a wonderful full-time job taking care of a Hasidic Jewish couple's baby boy. I can never take him outside because the air is not kosher. It's okay, their apartment has two rooms.'

-'I had to quit the babysitting job because I am too pregnant now.'

Edward and I had a beautiful son.
Then Dad had surgery to remove some faulty internal organs. He was very depressed at the loss. So I tried to cheer him up by talking about our old favorite topic, economics.
He turned the subject back to me. "For crying out loud, what are you doing with that boy?" He griped.
"We're married, Dad." I reminded him, trying to be helpful.
"In the Church?" he replied bitterly not needing an answer. He knew we had eloped which, to Catholics, was not valid. "And what ever happened to college?"
His words burned but I did not show any pain. I could not answer him without revealing all he did not know. I didn't have the will to break my silence to him or to anyone.
I did make an effort to explain how things had changed, but nothing I said eased his mind.

Eventually, he gathered that I could not go back to school or to the Church. I think I broke his heart.

So we didn't talk much after that.
Then I was so depressed my journals were almost suicidal.

When Dad finally died, my poems marked his passing.

Mourning For Nicholas
My kindred spirit
Has gone away
He does not speak
He cannot say
Where he is
Or where he'll be

Mine cannot follow
I cannot sleep
With wretched sorrow
With grief so deep
My kindred spirit
Has gone away

I didn't blame Mother or anyone for his death.

I believed it was just a part of life.

Seeing Mother at the funeral was not hard because I was still loyal to her. Christian was loyal too and he still despised me. The feeling was mutual. Even though I suppressed my hatred for him, the two of them still shut me out of their world.

At the time, I thought she was going along with what Christian wanted, just to keep the peace.

I accepted that she had to choose one of us, and that she chose him over me.

Yet, it was still harsh to feel so alone, like an orphan, when I wasn't.

So, I decided it was time to leave the cold. Edward suggested that we work our way down to the warmer climates.

I agreed, and we built a good life and a house with a lot of love and determination.

I rarely saw Mother after that, and we never spoke of the day I left home or why.

Part 4

Chapter 20
Burnt Christians

After reading the last entry of the last exiled journal, I noticed that it was 3 a.m. and I was sitting on the floor, with piles of my past all around me.

I looked up and was startled to see my gaunt face in the mirror. A dull pain in my stomach grew more severe. I realized I was hungry.

I suddenly got the urge to take care of me like a mother should. I smiled at myself with relief and glee. I got a jar of my favorite peanut butter and ate it as I carefully put all the journals chronologically back in their place.

I thought about the main reason I ventured back into my past, to find the source of Mom's itch.

I was satisfied that I had succeeded.

It all started the day of the rose bush attack. Since then, she behaved like a burnt Christian which my first grade teacher described long ago. Mom

evaded her guilt as best she could, by avoiding and silencing me, who was the only one, besides Christian, who witnessed her sins.
She aided a steady stream of needy people, as if helping them would count as penance for her actions that day.

When Christian abandoned her, she was all alone for the first time in her life. The maddening itch erupted as a sub-conscious, self-inflicted purgatory. Yet she persisted in her denial that it was all in her head.
She sought me out for help even while she hated that I could see what she was doing.
The self deceptive should never get close to the empathetic, who take notes on everything to avoid insanity.

I decided it would be futile to share my discovery of the cause of her mystery itch. Even though I had changed my mind about her, I knew she would not do the same about me.

Instead of admitting I was right, she would itch just to prove I was wrong.

Fortunately, I was beyond feeling hurt for that tactic. It was not important anymore.

In fact, I suddenly felt cured of my involuntary empathy, which, I realized, had given her easy access to all my sensitivities.

It was a relief to know that she could no longer crush me with just a few words.

Yet, I was mistaken to think the strange war between us was over.

This I confirmed the very next day when I heard her fall.

I rushed to her room and saw her spread out on the floor breathing hard. There were leaves in her mouth. I thought she was choking.

"I'm taking these leaves out of your mouth, Mother!" I told her firmly.

She did not resist but her eyes looked glazed.

"I'm calling an ambulance!" I stated.

"No," she said. "I'm alright."

She was well enough to get herself up off the floor without my help. I was about to scold her for scaring me but she started talking before I had a chance.

"Christian is dying." She said somberly. "I fell because I was overcome with grief."

The words did not register, and I wasn't sure I heard her right. I asked her to explain.

She replied sarcastically, "You don't know what the word 'dying' means?"

I said with a straight face, "So by 'dying' you mean Christian is crazy with a non-fatal, phantom disease?"

She frowned and said, "Don't make fun of my illness, June Marie."

"I'm not!" I laughed. "I'm *describing* your illness."

"That's not what I mean when I use that word," she pouted. "And you know it."

I was not going to argue with her so I asked, "Why do you think he's dying?"

She stated somberly, "He was running from the Catholic postal carrier and he fell into a kind of street machine. His kidneys were damaged badly."

Her explanation reeked of exaggeration and misinformation. I asked with no trace of alarm, "Do you mean he fell off his bike again and got hit by a car?"

"It wasn't like all those other times." She growled. "He wasn't riding his bike this time."

"Well is he 'dying' *today*?" I asked nonchalantly, convinced she was omitting key information.

"No." she said. "But he is on a list for a new kidney."

"Oh." I said, not believing her. "Then he isn't actually going to die, I mean not in the immediate future."

"He won't take anybody's kidney." She stated.

I thought for a moment. Since he opposed modern medicine as much as she did, then this was not surprising, if it was true. But I was pretty sure she was exaggerating.

Then I noticed she was watching me strangely and I started panicking. It suddenly occurred to me that if it was true, that he might be opposed to taking a kidney from *just anybody.*

I asked quickly, "Do you mean he would take a kidney if it was from a certain person, like a low- level relative, like me? Are you telling me this because you want *me* to give him one of *my* kidneys?!"

"No." she said with impatience. "And calm down. I mean he won't accept *any* kidney. So he has a few weeks or months before his starts to fail."

It took me a while to calm down and be sure that I was not being asked to donate an organ. Saying 'no' to her was still new to me. Then I digested her news.

Even though I only believed half of what she said about Christian, I wanted to know which half was true. I finally asked, "Why was Christian running from a mailman?"

"It was the postal police." She corrected me.

"Alright Mother,' I conceded. "Please explain what you are talking about."

She was satisfied of my sincerity and asked, "Do you remember what Christian does?"

Answering her question meant I had to think about Christian, which I normally loathed. But the recent light from my journal accounts caused my perception of him to be revised.

I knew he was still an ass, but I had to concede that he had been just as blindly loyal to Mother as I was. We both craved the favor of her pious authority, with no thought of the price. No matter how much our mother declared his innocence, he knew in his heart that he owed reparations for his offenses to us. Yet he could not bring himself to apologize to those he thought were beneath him. The conflict tormented him and he must have guessed it would only get worse if he became a priest. The church would overlook his weaknesses just as Mother had. He closed the door to the seminary but went on to act like a priest anyway. He never married and he remained celibate.

This choice led him to unwittingly start a 'harsh on himself' missionary service for the sick and dying.

Obviously an apology to us would have been less grueling than the hellish life he chose as part of his self-imposed penance.

She interrupted my thoughts with a poke of her grabber stick. "Are you deaf?" She asked sarcastically.
"No, Mother." I replied annoyed.
She grabbed for some papers and said, "Then please explain to me what Christian does."

I put my thoughts of Christian aside, and simply replied, "He visits the old people."

"And he does so much good for them," She gushed as if he was a saint already.

"Alright Mother," I rushed her. "I answered you now tell me the rest of this drama."

She frowned and continued, "Well, sometimes, lately a lot of the time, he can't ride his bike. So he rides around with Father Phil, who is blind and has occasional seizures but has a van."

I recalled the name but didn't believe her description. So I asked, "How do you know for sure that Father Phil is blind?

"I saw he was blind the *very first time* I met him!" she scoffed.

"Alright," I growled, "but how do you know he drives?"

"He and Christian gave me a ride to the 'All India' store for my Neem leaves" she chirped. "And I saw that Christian was telling Father Phil when to turn and when he's getting too close to the ditch. Sometimes he'll hold the wheel when Father Phil is having 'an episode'."

It sounded so ridiculous I was sure she was exaggerating. Yet if it was even a little true, it was alarming and I said, "That doesn't sound safe at all."

"Yeah, that's what I've been saying," she replied. "Christian admits it isn't the safest way to get around. But since they only travel for church business, Father Phil says that Jesus has to watch out for them. Here is his card."

She handed me a little insurance card that showed a giant Jesus standing over a highway with the caption, 'I will cover all your sins and insurance needs.'

I commented. "There is no phone number on this card, Mother. And the address is handwritten on the back."

She replied sincerely, "That's Father Phil's address and you have to 'pray' for coverage."

I asked in my fake/sincere voice, "Would Jesus really recognize a trip to the 'All India' store as legitimate church business?"

She quickly answered, "I am sure at one time, Jesus walked to India and talked to the swamis."

"Don't change the subject, Mother," I said sternly, as I suppressed a giggle. "And don't try to defraud Jesus because you will fail."

She frowned at me and continued her summary. "They took me to the India store because it was on their church-business route."

"They have a route?" I asked.

"Yes," she said. "Together they give communion to all the shut-ins who can't make it to mass. As a side job, they collect usable junk they find and store it on Father Phil's junk farm, just outside the city."

It sounded like she was taking the long way around to get to some point. So I again rushed her along, "That is all typically strange, but what are you really trying to say?"

She sighed and said dramatically, "Of course, when the weather is too hazardous, Father Phil won't drive the van."

"Okay," I pestered. "So what happens then?"

She said slowly, "So Father Phil tells Christian that he should give communion."

That sounded unlikely and I asked, "Does the Church allow that?"

"Lay clergy can, yes." She said with hesitation.

I was impatient, "Okay mom, Christian is a lay Clergy right?"

"Yes," she said, "But without a sanctioned priest present, it's like impersonating a priest. Christian is afraid of being excommunicated for that."

"Well of course," I agreed. "but isn't Father Phil present for the communion?"

"Well," she said timidly. "When Father Phil can't be there, Christian gets him to bless the stack of wafers first, and then he mails the Eucharist to the shut-ins."

It was getting so nuts I said, "I don't think Christian does that, Mother. Its too risky and he is not an idiot."

She was quick with her response. "But he *has* been mailing Eucharist to parishioners! He even sends them to me, ever since I left Wisconsin and he found out you were *not* taking me to mass."

She was trying to make me feel guilty but I was immune.

I persisted with my argument and said, "He probably gets an extra Eucharist on Sunday and then just sends it to you, Mother."

She just looked at me in silence.

I continued, "It can't be catholically legal or ethical to run a mail-order communion operation. Think of the complaints from the parishioners who have to go to the church to get communion!"

To my surprise she said, "But Father Phil is the one supplying the hosts and he blesses them in batches."

I didn't expect that answer and was curious. I asked, "How big are the batches?"

"Oh I guess they send out 100's every week during the winter." She replied casually.

I was baffled and exclaimed, "That must get expensive to mail all those Eucharist! Does the church pay for postage?"

"No," she replied, "At least I don't think so because I don't think the church knows about it."

I was even more baffled. "How could the church *not* know one of their priests is giving out 100s of Eucharist a week?"

"Well," she said with a frown, "Father Phil gets some of his holy supplies from discount dealers."

"There are discount dealers of Eucharist?" I laughed.

She replied sincerely, "Well they are only communion wafers until they are blessed. Then they become Eucharist. I can understand why you have forgotten that, you've been wandering around in this wilderness for so long."

I ignored her bait again, and quickly asked, "Why doesn't he get them from the church?"

"Well because the church won't give him that many Eucharist!" she protested.

I was getting impatient to get to the bottom of this odd arrangement. "*Why* won't they give one of their priests enough communion wafers to meet the needs of the parish?"

"Because Father Phil doesn't officially have a parish. He is a substitute priest now."

"Why doesn't he have a parish? "I asked sternly, and with expectation of a scandalous answer.

"Because he drives around in a van, and he is too blind." She finally admitted. "The church wants him to stop that, but he's stubborn and won't retire to the Mother House. He wants to stay on the farm he grew up on. So they won't let him have a parish."

Separating fact from fiction was exhausting. I carefully attempted to summarize the strange drama she described.

I stated, "So Father Phil and Christian have started an unsanctioned Catholic fringe church that is giving possibly counterfeit communion to alleged shut-ins, sometimes via the mail. "

"You don't have to make it sound so criminal." She pouted.

I was suddenly curious about that possibly criminal point and asked, "How do they get away with not paying postage?"

"Christian does the mailing and doesn't use new stamps. That's why I have to send these back to him."

That's when I noticed she was cutting the stamps off the mail we received. I was completely dumbfounded.

"How can he use used stamps?" I asked incredulously. "Doesn't the USPS just reject them?!"

"I guess not" she replied unconcerned as she kept cutting.

"He's been doing this for a long time."

"But he gets donations, money, from the people he gives communion to, right?" I asked.

"Yes." She replied unconcerned. "Sometimes."

"So why can't he just use that money to buy stamps?" I asked. "Why risk trouble with the postal system?"

"Christian *won't* buy new stamps." She said with some annoyance at all my questions.

"Why?" I asked.

"For the same reason he won't get a drivers license." She replied stubbornly. "He's refuses to support war."

"How is war related to stamps?" I asked with growing fatigue and skepticism. I knew Christian still had a short temper, which was inconsistent with the conventional anti-war philosophy of 'peace and love'.

She replied simply, "The postal service is funded by loans from the federal government. Buying stamps funds war on the potential Catholic converts."

I sighed at the convoluted thinking

that went into the whole scheme. My head was aching from it.

I finally stated, "So he's been ripping off both the United States Postal Service and the Catholic church."

"Well yes." She said quietly. "And they finally caught up with him, just as he feared."

"How did they catch him?" a variety of scenarios raced through my mind, but I waited for her answer.

She replied, "A Catholic Crimes Investigator was posing as postal carrier so he could follow Christian."

"Was it a Jesuit CCI?" I asked with concern.

"Thankfully no, so he was unarmed." She replied. "The CCI confronted Christian at an old post office on the edge of town, and asked to inspect the batch of Eucharist Christian was trying to mail. He was not very nice about it, according to Christian."

She was getting slow so I encouraged her to finish quickly "So what did Christian do?"

"Christian panicked, threw the box of Eucharist away, and ran into traffic without looking."

"You said he ran into a 'street machine'." I commented.

"Oh did I?" she floundered. "Well I meant traffic. Cars are kind of like street machines."

Her answer made the story sound even more contrived, but I was willing to play along if I could get even a few facts out of her.

I asked, "How much traffic could there be at an old rural post office?"

"Well," she clearly wanted to avoid answering. "It wasn't really that much traffic."

"How many cars, Mother?" I persisted.

"There were no cars." she grumbled. "There was just one van."

I stared at her for a few moments, trying really hard not to laugh. Finally I asked, "Was there a blind priest driving it?"

"Yes!" she sobbed. "It was Father Phil driving the getaway van! He was supposed to be the lookout! I warned Christian that one day Father Phil would kill him!"

Her response was quite unexpected. She seemed genuinely upset and actually relieved to be getting the burdensome saga out of her system. So I kept asking questions. "Why would Father Phil drive off without Christian in the van?"

She gulped as she closed her eyes and pursed her lips. Finally she replied, "Well, it was probably parked, in the parking lot, and Christian was in such a hurry to get away from the mail-man spy that he crashed right into the van. Father Phil heard the thud, and opened the door to let Christian in."

"And how were his kidneys damaged from that?" I asked dramatically pressuring her to give the truth.

She struggled to explain, "Christian was so dazed from hitting the side of the van so hard that he fell down."

I waited, with arms folded, for her to finish. She continued with great awkwardness. "His head bumped the collection of junk they keep on the van rack. The junk fell down on top of him. Some of them simply crushed his kidney, both of them I mean. That is all there is to it. I have nothing more to confess."

I don't know why the truth was worse than what she was making up. But I played along anyway, by offering my own made up scenario.

I proceeded like I was Sherlock Holmes. "Is it possible that Father Phil had the engine running to keep warm that night?"

"Yes, I suppose so." She said quietly whimpering.

"And could he have been so startled by the thud of Christian crashing into the van," I continued. "That he accidentally bumped the gear into reverse, causing the van to move backwards?" She whimpered more and I kept going. "Is it possible that Father Phil ran backwards over Christian, in the parking lot and that is how his kidney was crushed?"

She was sobbing for a long time before she finally stated, "Yes, yes! How did you know?"

I was surprised I was right and curious about how I deduced it.

After I paused to think, I said, "It's not very likely that some old junk falling on Christian could do that much damage. He's always been a durable person and has survived worse than that. Also, since you've said that Christian has frequently been injured in traffic, it seems likely that this has happened before, and probably with Father Phil."

She bawled loudly, "Yes! Father Phil hits Christian with the van all the time!"

"Why?" I asked with astonishment.

"Because he's blind!" she howled. "And because Christian keeps forgiving him! They both should have been dead a long time ago! I've told Christian he should stop hanging around with blind clerics! But he is too stupidly loyal to men of God! He doesn't' know what's bad for him!" she sobbed.

It was not funny of course, so I did not laugh, out loud, while she was sobbing, for Christian.
However I found it wickedly comical that Christian should end up being so painfully loyal to an angel of death like Father Phil.

Chapter 21
Hemlock And Curry

Of course Mom wanted to see the allegedly 'dying' Christian as soon as possible.

We were on the plane to Wisconsin the next day.

After we were seated in the plane, I noticed she pulled out some strange looking fresh leaves.

"Where did those come from?" I asked.

"You planted them for me remember?" she said.

"No." I replied. "When did I do that?"

"It was months ago when you used to be nice."

I sighed at her cut but did not respond.

She continued, "It was when you planted all those plants we bought."

"Oh yes." I said as I remembered the stupid fight we had so long ago.

I was such a child then, last year.

It was ridiculous that I thought I had to pay for my anger by helping her with 'gardening'.

I was so relieved that those days were done and gone. My loyalty to her was more than fulfilled.

I was ready to sever any remaining ties to my cobra-like mother. She could still be lethal and hurt me in ways I could not imagine.

I knew she never truly intended to be harmful to anyone.

I had finally accepted that my mother was just a happy, selfish, passive-aggressive, weapon of destruction, whom I would always love unconditionally, but only from a safe distance, and when fully armed.

She didn't realize it, but this trip to Wisconsin would be her last.

I had decided that I was going to finish the book about money, just like I should have done 25 years earlier. I wanted to do it for myself and to keep my promise to Dad. It would never get written if I had to live with a cobra. So I planned to find her a place.

This time I would not leave until she was safely exiled in someone else's jurisdiction.

To be discreet and sensitive, I would not say anything about it until after we met with Christian.

As I plotted my abandonment of her, I was still examining one of the leaves she had brought.

It seemed vaguely familiar and I said to her "This doesn't look like anything we bought."

"These are Neem leaves." she said quickly and pulled it away from me. "We got these on the upland edge of the bog."

"Those are not Neem leaves mother." I said with increasing alarm. "And you know it."

"You should know what they are, you gave them to me." She snapped.

"Yeah," I replied. "And I know these aren't Neem. Why won't you just tell me the name?"

"It doesn't matter what you call them because they stop my itching." She said adamantly and put them away. "Thank you for supplying me my medicine."

It was pointless to fight with her, especially on the plane. So I tried to forget about it, but it kept nagging me. My mind wandered to that day we walked out to the bog.

The outing was strange because, even then, she acted like she could not remember the name of the plant she was looking for. I was more annoyed because I got hit by an avocado pit that a squirrel dropped on me from above.

It was not a pleasant time to revisit.

So I stopped thinking about it. Soon I would be totally free of her, and those wretched Neem and curry leaves forever.

After the plane landed we went right to the hospital to see Christian, whom I had not personally seen in decades. I had seen a few photos of him over the

years, but I still did not recognize him. He really did look like he had been repeatedly run over by a van.
I felt ashamed for ever hating him.

After awhile I realized he had been watching me, like he didn't know for sure who I was. I didn't enlighten him.
Finally he waved feebly at me and under his thick beard a smile formed. It was crowded out by the wince of severe pain.
I waved back at him, feeling only the eternity between us.
He spoke in a quiet raspy voice, "I'm sorry that Edward is leaving you but it's for the better."
I guess he knew who I was after all. I repressed my urge to smack him even as I looked around for a whacking device.
He continued, "And thank you for bringing Mom back home where she belongs."
I nodded with extreme restraint, as I eyed up the tubes attached to his nose that maybe helped him breathe.

"Oh, you're welcome," I said distracted. Then I asked curiously, "How do you know she is staying here?"

"Didn't she tell you?" He wheezed in pain.

I really wanted to know what he meant, but it caused him so much anguish to talk, I let it go. Instead I replied, "Oh, yes, I guess she did."

I figured that she probably had already arranged to leave us, which would be so nice.

I was done serving her.

I contemplated all the events that led me to here, to his bedside.

Observing him so closely made me see how badly damaged he was. I was about to ask him if he really got run over by Father Phil, but then Mom stepped in front of me.

She smiled her warm comforting smile that I had grown to fear. She sat next to him and held his hand, an action that used to convince me that I was about to have my spirit crushed.

I shuddered and waited outside the door. They deserved each other. They talked for hours like two little kids talking about their simple lives. This time there was no yelling, no ranting.

Then I was deeply saddened because it felt like an unhappy ending. It seemed wrong that Mom had to outlive her favorite son. She always wanted to die with all her children around, trying to help her.

As I waited, a man dressed in black suddenly appeared. He looked at the room number and asked me if I was a relative of the patient. I said "Yes, I'm his sister."

Then he handed me a 'postage due' letter. Christian owed the United States Postal Service $558.00.

"If he ever wakes up, tell him that I'll get all charges dropped if he pays the bill and reveals who gave him the communion wafers."

"I heard it was a discount dealer." I said trying to be helpful as I looked for clues that he was a CCI. I had never met one before.

"There is no such thing." He scowled. "Tell him to contact me before it's too late. He has a lot of explaining to do."

He gave me his card and disappeared down a dark hallway. I wondered what he meant.

My thoughts were interrupted as the nurse came to spread a salty concoction on Christian's wounds.

I could tell from his groans that it burned. When I heard him explaining to Mom why he refused any other less painful remedy, I opted to find a less nauseating place to wait.

Unfortunately Mom soon found me and sunk into the cozy chair next to mine. So I left her alone to get some peanuts. I was ravenously hungry.

When I got back I noticed she was still there. Her breathing was sporadic so I shook her up a bit and some of those leaves dropped out of her mouth.

I froze because, at that moment, I suddenly remembered the name of the plant.

It was Hemlock.

I shook her awake.

Her eyes rolled around in their sockets.

"Wake up! Mother! "I yelled. "You have to wake up now!"

She murmured as I shook her.

"I've done all I could." She mumbled

"No!" I panicked. I sobbed. "No mother! I love you please don't go! I need you!"

"No, girl," She smiled. "You can go now. I want to set you free."

"You are not doing this to me!" I yelled and then added "and blaming me for your death *is* **not** setting me free!"

She didn't comment, but she did look very peaceful, like a death sleep was approaching.

"Nurse!" I yelled. "She needs her stomach pumped!"

The nurse rushed to me. I handed her the leaves

"She took Hemlock!" I yelled.

The nurse simply stared at me.

"It's a poisonous plant! It can cause asphyxiation. She can't breathe!" I screamed.

The nurse finally sprung into action. They rushed Mom to the emergency room. I called all my siblings to come right away, back to the hospital where Christian was.

After what seemed like an eternity, a doctor came out to speak with me.

"She can breathe now." He said.

I was relieved. "Thank you doctor," I said fumbling over my words. "I'm sorry about this. She didn't tell me. It's a weird story."

He got right to the point and asked, "Where did she get Hemlock from?"

I froze up again and then fumbled awkwardly, "I um... we live in Florida. She knows a lot about plants. She just acts senile but I know better. She asked for it. We had a fight and I lost, so I got her these plants. I didn't know what Hemlock was. I mean I knew it was poisonous, everyone does. I just gave her what she wanted. You see,

I was really angry back then, but I'm okay now. Is she okay too?"

"No." the doctor said. "The Hemlock and something else damaged her liver. She could be put on a list, but she said she would refuse it. She says she's lived long enough."

The news did not alarm me in any way. I had heard about her death so often that it had become meaningless. I was sure that as soon as this doctor found out the truth about Mom's habits, that he would revise his diagnosis.

So I just smiled and nodded at his statement which, I noticed, alarmed him. I couldn't think of the appropriate words of grief because I didn't feel any. Then I panicked.

It occurred to me that he was waiting for signs of sorrow from me because I was implicated in attempts to poison my mother with the Hemlock! I already admitted where I got it from and that I gave it to her, after a fight!

That's when I imagined my own trial for attempted murder. Her victory over me would be complete.

Emotionally, it was too much to take. With low blood-sugar from not eating enough peanuts and right there in front of the doctor, I fainted.

When I woke up in the comfy chair, the nurses and doctors were conveniently absent. So I rushed in to see Mom. Since she was still alive, I was determined to make her clear me of wrongdoing.

She looked up at me, smiled sweetly and said, "I'm not itching. That plant worked."

"That plant is killing you." I whispered harshly, "and it could end up killing me too."

"Well," She casually replied, "we all have to go someday."

I was annoyed with her casual dismissal of my possible death. So I reminded her of her duty. "Well it's a sin to make that choice for yourself and for others, including me!"

"I didn't sin." She looked offended.

"You took Hemlock, Mother," I countered. "That I gave you!"

"For my itching!" she stated emphatically as she wheezed.

I challenged her statement and asked. "You didn't know that Hemlock could cause fatal asphyxiation?"

"Well the kind that grows where Socrates lived can." she responded with great clarity. "But there are many kinds of Hemlock, and they don't all have the same potency."

She was correct of course. Even on her alleged deathbed the woman was still sharp as broken glass.

"I want you to tell *that* to the doctor. " I said sternly. "He thinks I had something to do with your damaged liver."

"My liver?" she said curiously. "I think those curry leaves damaged my liver."

"No mother, "I replied very annoyed. "Even though you know how much I despise those curry leaves, we both know you can't die from them."

"Well Christian found out that they were coated with coal tar powder to preserve their freshness." She stated plainly. Then she laughed, "We've both been sucking on gas."

As usual, I proceeded to translate all her words. All that was initially registering was joy that she was finally admitting the 'curry' leaves were not 'Neem'.

For the rest of it, I had to think what was true and what was for dramatic effect.

Even after a half hour, the full impact of what she was saying had still not hit me. My dendrites were so slow.

It was not even surprising that the leaves were doused in a petroleum by-product. They always reeked of something like diesel fuel. If she was really sucking on them, then she could, maybe, die from them, I supposed.

Then something did hit me; a memory hit me.

I demanded of her, "*When,* exactly, did Christian tell you there was petroleum on those leaves?"

She frowned, "I don't know, and what does it matter now anyway?"

"Because you tried to make *me* take those leaves when I was... was not eating." I stated with a tone of firm accusation.

"Did I?" she acted innocent. "Well, I'm sorry if I got the leaves mixed up, I can't remember everything."

It was pointless to argue with her, but I was certain she had tried to get me to eat those tainted leaves.

The truth slowly sunk in that my mother had probably been trying to silence me by killing me with curry leaves! The evidence could easily convict her.

I was briefly saddened, as I imagined the somber scenario of charging my mother for attempted homicide.

Then I thought of the Hemlock again, and realized that I could not charge her for any kind of murder because she would just counter-charge me.

She was so good she would probably win. Even if she confessed to murder, no one would believe her or, if they did, they would still not convict her because she would act all crazy.

So I decided to let go of the whole 'curry-leaf assassination attempt' problem. It was easier to forgive her anyway.

I hugged her and said, "I love you mother. I'm sorry I could not follow you to…" I turned away to hide my lack of sincerity, "your death."

"Oh that's alright," she replied happily, which confirmed that she knew she wasn't actually dying. "At least my itching has stopped."

Her mention of the itch reminded me of my secret discovery.

Since she was admitting that she no longer itched, and she was on a fake deathbed, I thought this might be an opportunity to get some credit for discovering the source of her itch. It was even possible that she would confess her guilt.

I turned back to her and said sweetly, "Mother, do you remember when your itching first started?"

"What does it matter now?" she asked.

"Well, I've thought a lot about it" I replied. "I think I know when."

"Really?" she smirked. "Why should you know?"

"Because I was there that day." I said.

"What day was that?" she asked.

"It was when you got badly scratched by the rose bush. Remember?" I responded coolly and then added. "And I know you saw what Christian did to me."

Her face grew white. There was no need for empathy to know exactly what she was feeling. Her eyes closed, and her breathing got sporadic, like she was dying.

I did not respond to the diversionary tactic. She could not maintain it.

"I forgive you Mother" I said calmly. Finally she opened her eyes.

"For what?!" she suddenly snapped. "I did nothing wrong *that* day!"

"You didn't punish him for what he tried to do to me." I replied. "Not ever."

She scoffed "Ha! You didn't mind letting it go all these years either! Maybe you wanted me to let him scare you into doing what was right! You never said anything to anyone!"

I gulped at those words and with pained restraint conceded, "I agree that my silence was a mistake, Mother. But I paid dearly for that. I miss him every day and wish I could tell him I'm sorry." I had to pause briefly to remember him and then added quietly, "What you permitted went beyond mere silence."

She paused too before evasively retaliating, "Maybe Christian went too far sometimes, but only because you did what you pleased! You were never as loyal as he was! He was a good son!

I'm glad I chose him!"

That hurt too but I sucked it up and asked quietly, "Why did you need to choose one or the other?"

"You two didn't get along." She replied flippantly.

I retorted, "That doesn't explain anything! Why couldn't you help me with school and why did you always have to crush my spirit?"

She huffed, "Oh, well, I'm not perfect. I can't do everything."

I balked at that and shot back with the real reason. "And you didn't like it that I knew you so well. You didn't want me talking and ruining your reputation."

"I live my life as I please." she growled. "Why should I care what anyone thinks of me?"

"Because if they think badly of you then they won't volunteer to serve you, loyally as we did for so long!" I stated correctly. "And you were running out of servants. You lost your last one when Christian finally did quit 18 months ago, completely burned by you."

"Why should any of that cause itching now?" she seemed genuinely curious.

I hesitated as I tried to think of the best way to explain my theory.

Finally I said, "Because you are a Christian."

"And that causes itching?" she laughed.

I scowled and stated, "Avoiding guilt, confession, and penance will give you hives. Sister Magdelyn told us that if you didn't go to confession and you didn't do penance then you would be haunted by your sin."

She closed her eyes and was quiet for a long time.

"Like Lady Macbeth?" she finally said with eyes still closed.

"Well, yes," I replied, amused that she was comparing herself to a homicidal queen. "And it nags you until you do penance for it."

She opened her eyes and said hopefully, "Or until you die and are forgiven?"

"Yes, I suppose so, "I responded carefully. " But I think you have already done penance for this."

"You mean this itch?" she asked.

"Yes," I replied. "I think, after all these years, you've finally judged yourself guilty. You made me and Christian your jury. The itch is your execution, even if it's really just in your head"

She was lost in thought. Finally she said, "I guess it would have been easier to just say I'm sorry."

It was the closest to an actual apology I had ever heard from her. I viewed it as congratulations for my correct answer. I was satisfied, but not for long.

She pulled me out of my revelry with a cough and a hand motion to come closer to her.

"There is something I want you to know, June Marie." She said very quietly.

"What is it?" I said with uncertainty.

She sighed somberly, "I want to tell you how my brother Luke died."

Chapter 22
The Angel of Death

Of course I already knew that story. Yet she seemed determined to tell it again, so I sat down to listen.

"That day Luke died," She began, "I said that he was supposed to take care of me."

"Yes." I sighed with disappointment because it seemed she intended to relay the whole sorry saga again. I could be sitting there for an hour or more.

So I did my best to discourage the performance "I know Mother, you think you did it." I said with compassion. "It's okay. I'm sure everyone forgives you."

Her eyes were damp with tears as she said. "I was supposed to take care of him."

"What?" I was confused. "Who were you supposed to take care of?"

She continued, "Mother took me aside that day to ask *me* to take care of Luke."

"Why would she do that?" I asked.

She sobbed, "Because I was bigger and stronger than Luke, and he was... sick, or stunted, or I don't remember what illness he had. Anyway, he couldn't care for me anymore, not like he used to. Ma didn't want to embarrass Luke by asking one of the boys to look after him. She made me agree to watch him if I wanted to go swimming. So I was mad."

There was no need to translate her words. It was plain that all of what she said was true.

"What did you do?" I asked with a sick feeling.

She replied quickly. "I rushed ahead of Luke, to get away from him, and I jumped in. Luke followed too closely, so I... kicked him away."

I thought about the sorry event and then added, "Then he struggled in the current and you didn't help."

"I didn't think it was my job to help him. He was older and always cared for *me*." She pouted. "It was stupid of mother to expect a girl to be of any use. So I started gasping for air like I was drowning."

"What did you think that would do?" I asked, confused.

"If they thought I was drowning too," she said defiantly. "Then they wouldn't blame me for his death."

"You were thirteen, Mother." I said.

She scoffed, "I was an adult in the eyes of God. Everyone knew that."

It was an odd reason and I asked, "So you thought you could evade the eyes of God?"

"His judgment will come when I die and I know God will understand my point of view." She said confidently. "I didn't want my family and the town to judge me while I was living."

Her confession was silly and sad.

Yet it revealed that she still struggled with the guilt of *that* awful day, which, in her mind, dwarfed the sin of the 'rose bush' day. I could also see that guilt for her brother's death had profoundly altered her life, and the lives of her children. Thankfully, it was for a crime that required no human action. She'd have to settle it with her maker. It was not my concern. Even though I didn't care anymore, I was still polite enough to respond appropriately.

I finally said quietly, "Mother, I think this is something you should confess to a priest."

"Yes," she said kindly, "That's why I want you to give my confession to Christian for me. You are such a good little helper, and you understand me so well."

"Christian isn't a priest." I said with confusion.

She replied sincerely. "He can act on Father Phil's behalf."

"Priests can't outsource confessions Mother!" I protested and then added quickly, "or last rites!"

"Well they can outsource communion!" she countered, and then dramatically gasped for air.

I was annoyed and snapped, "You don't even seem that sorry!"

She snapped, "I'm sorry Luke didn't live longer! But mother shouldn't have made me responsible for taking care of her children. God knows I was too young for that. I was only thirteen!"

Her sudden change of perspective made me dizzy, but I challenged her anyway.

"I took care of the twins when I was five!" I protested.

"I didn't *make you* do that." she wheezed. "You *wanted* to do that!"

"Only because that was how I got love and praise from you!" I stated.

"You got praise from me for *that*?" she breathed heavily. "For always interfering with things?"

With those few apathetic words, and even as she was apparently breathing her last, she was able to utterly crush me. I was defenseless against her because she was dying and I was not. So it was an unfair fight.

So I put some sleeping pills in her water. I emoted as I helped her drink it saying, "Now that you know that I know that you have been crushing me my whole life, I just want to say that I *still* love you unconditionally."

The pills were kicking in pretty fast so she couldn't respond much.

She did manage to whisper sweetly, "Just tell Christian I'm leaving this world now. It will make him happy to know I'm going to heaven."

I struggled to control my gag as I said quietly, "I will tell him."

I didn't bother to explain that it was the pills, and not death, that were making her unconscious.

I was also miffed that he would be the topic of her dying words.

Mom was still sleeping when all my siblings had arrived. So I filled them in on what happened as best I could. It was hard to follow.

I concluded with a straight face, "She is dying of course."

There was a somber silence for awhile. Then they all started giggling.

The comedy spiraled out of control after I explained that Hemlock grows wild in Florida, and that Mom's medicinal curry leaves were dusted with coal tar.

Over the din of guffawing I explained that Christian was so afraid of excommunication for himself and for Father Phil that he refuses to tell the Catholic Crimes Investigator anything about the discount communion dealer or the source of the tainted curry.

I had to insist that I was not exaggerating. Of course no one believed Mother was actually on her way out. They did all cheer at the news of the liver damage which could easily get her into long term care.

Then Mark asked why the curry leaves were soaked in gas.

"I assumed that coal tar was a tradition of India," I stated.

They all said 'no', and that I was crazy for thinking that.

Then Mike added, "Sometimes oil soaked leaves make good wicks in oil lamps."

Mark agreed and said, "I saw a few kerosene lamps lying around at Father Phil's farm, when I was out there to fix his sink."

Madeline stated, "So Father Phil was Christian's supplier of tainted curry."

Paul shook his head and asked, "Why would Father Phil have kerosene lamps if he's blind?"

Mark laughed and said, "Father Phil is not blind."

"Mom said he was." I countered.

He retorted, "Well the Father Phil I met read a work order out loud."

We all stood there stunned with mouths gaping at the revelation.

Finally I said, "Mom complained that Father Phil was going to kill Christian with the van someday, while doing God's work."

Madeline stated with a straight face, "So Father Phil was just another angel of death?"

I nodded and said, "It was probably his mission to run over sinners with his van."

Paul dismissed that idea and said, "He's a dangerous lunatic, and we have to stop him. Do you remember how to get to the farm, Mark?"

Mark hesitated and said, "I'm not sure."

"I've got his address!" I said as I pulled out the 'Jesus insurance' card and handed it to Mark.

He laughed as he read the card and said, "Come on June, give me the card with the address."

"Oh I'm sorry," I said sarcastically. "Try turning the card over. It's written on the back."

"Nope," He said playfully as he showed me the card. "Still useless, but funny."

Mike jabbed him as he was waiting for the address. I finally had to say, "It was on this card when Mom gave it to me."

Mark grinned, "So you don't have the card with the address. That's just great."

"I'm really sorry." I was sincerely dumbfounded.

"Don't worry about it." Mike said, "He can remember the way if we feed him pizza first."

We all agreed and after eating, we followed Mark through the winding country roads.

We found an elderly blind man living at the farm, but his name was Old Joe, and Mark had never seen him before.

He greeted us nicely and then we explained that Christian was in the hospital. He was sad about that but answered our questions.

He stated, "Father Phil was my uncle, he lived here, and he owned that van over by the barn. But like I told the other fella who was here asking the same things, Uncle Phil died 25 years ago."

Mark asked, "Well, do you know who Christian rode with to get to the farm?"

Old Joe replied, "Christian always came here alone."

We were all curious about how a blind man could know if Christian was alone. Old Joe guessed our question and said, "I'm not deaf, just blind."

"Who was the other fella you said was here?" I asked politely.

Old Joe suddenly laughed, "He said he was from the United States Postal Service! But he sounded like a CCI to me."

Mark asked if he had any kerosene lamps. Old Joe led us to the van. It was filled with chickens. Kerosene lamps were on the ground next to it. The wicks were leaves. I confirmed that they were curry.

Paul asked, "What are the kerosene lamps for?"

Old Joe replied helpfully, "Christian brought those to give a little bit of heat to the chickens. You can have 'em. I don't know what he's been burning in them, but it stinks bad."

We chatted with Old Joe for awhile longer. He invited us to return any time. He liked visitors. We departed feeling more bewildered than ever by the mysterious discovery.

We visited Christian at the hospital again, and hoped he would give us clues about Father Phil.

He said nothing revealing, still afraid of the CCI.

It didn't matter. The damage was done. Mom and Christian both had irreversible liver damage, in addition to Christian's failing kidneys. Neither would accept a donated organ. There were no other options.

The only natural and effective remedy available to ease pain was medicinal marijuana, which Christian reluctantly agreed to. The combination of physiology, organ damage, and age made them extremely mellow, dazed, or asleep.

When Christian was sufficiently conscious, Paul told him that Mom was gone.

Christian looked so relieved, as if he had been just waiting for her to leave us. He said he was ready to go to heaven too.

No one mentioned that Mom was 'gone' because the hospital somehow lost her. Even though we were sure she was in no danger, we searched everywhere with no sign of our elusive mother. Of course none of us was that eager to find her.

Days later rumors started that Father Phil secretly took her for a ride in his van. It was a plausible explanation and it was comforting to think they were together, maybe searching for burnt Christians who were avoiding penance.

In any case, we all expected that she would call soon enough.

She'll probably say she was waiting for us on Norwich. I probably won't answer.

The End

Made in the USA
San Bernardino, CA
01 December 2015